Praise for Donna Alward's *The Girl Most Likely*

"...a story of with all human elements. The need to be loved, the fear of failure and being scared to put yourself out there in case of rejection. But it's also about keeping faith and seeing people for who they really are."

~ *Janet Davies, Once Upon A Romance*

The Girl Most Likely

Donna Alward

A SAMHAIN PUBLISHING, LTD. publication.

Samhain Publishing, Ltd.
2932 Ross Clark Circle, #384
Dothan, AL 36301
www.samhainpublishing.com

The Girl Most Likely
Copyright © 2006 by Donna Alward
Print ISBN: 1-59998-343-5
Digital ISBN: 1-59998-140-8

Editing by Jessie Bimberg
Cover by Scott Carpenter

First Samhain Publishing, Ltd. electronic publication: September 2006
First Samhain Publishing, Ltd. print publication: December 2006

Dedication

To D, my real life hero.

Chapter One

Katie wiped her sweating hands on her skirt, lifted her hand to knock on the dark wooden door, and drew it back.

For the third time.

Why was she afraid of seeing Richard Emerson again? They hadn't seen each other since high school. Surely they'd both grown up enough to leave unpleasantness behind. But the stakes were higher now, at least for her. Richard was her last chance, as far as she could tell. She'd been standing before his office door for five full minutes and had yet to garner the courage to knock.

Before she could chicken out once more, she took a deep breath, rapped on the closed door three times, and stepped back. She tugged at her navy skirt and matching jacket, hoping she looked professional.

"Come in," a deep voice intoned, and she turned the knob. It was slippery in her palm and she exhaled, trying, but failing to calm the nerves bouncing around in the pit of her stomach.

Stepping into the office, she saw him sitting in a seating area on the left. Richard, dark and imposing, ensconced in a comfortable blue chair, files before him on a glass-topped round table.

"I'll be right with you," he said, without looking up.

She couldn't help but stare. Where was the lanky, nerdy boy she remembered? The man with the thick file before him was no geek. His hair was rich and black with a hint of natural curl, and the sleeves of his dress shirt were rolled back to reveal strong forearms sprinkled with dark hair. Her eyes widened and pulse quickened at the sight of the man he'd become.

She forced herself to divert her attention to his office and she was further discomfited by the startling neatness and the precision of organization. Honeyed hardwood covered the floors. A gigantic bookshelf covered one wall, each book spine lined up neatly. There was a beige file cabinet to a side, a smooth dark desk, and a plush leather chair empty behind it. Everything was in an exact place...she wagered if she asked him where his extra staples were, he'd pull them out of a slot made specifically for that very purpose. All indications pointed to an orderly, analytical mind. In that way, she supposed, he hadn't changed.

She heard the file close.

"Sorry about that, Miss..."

"Katie..."

His head turned. "Buick," he finished, his lips curving up a bit in surprised recognition. "My God. It is you. Dad said you might be dropping by."

"Yes, on business."

She wiped her hands on her skirt again, cursing inwardly at her awkwardness.

For a long moment they stared at each other. She saw his eyes were the same dark brown, still fringed with thick lashes. They had always been his best feature. She counted back. Ten years ago, they'd graduated. Ten years ago, he'd been the one with sweaty palms, and he'd invited her to the prom. Ten years ago, she'd laughed in his face. Not that he'd helped matters any. He'd had scrawny arms and a pimply face and was generally known as a complete nerd. Still, they'd had a few classes together and their parents were friends. He wasn't bad to talk to. And he'd had big dreams. Katie'd admired that.

But he'd waited until three days before prom to ask her, and then he'd done it in public around all her friends. They'd never understood that Katie actually liked Nerdboy, as they'd called him then. One of the girls...she couldn't even remember her name now...had made a snotty remark, and Katie had done something cruel—she'd laughed at him. Instantly, his cheeks had stained red and he'd shuffled away. She'd felt awful, but had never got up the courage to apologize.

Now the joke was on her.

The man rising before her had certainly changed; his dark looks were now quite handsome. He'd lost his gawky teenage gangliness and his face was clear and tanned, smooth from his morning shave. His legs extended as he stood—long and lean in the expensive fabric of his suit—while his shirt stretched taut across broad shoulders. In fact, besides the eyes and the shape of his mouth, it was almost like looking at a different person. He came forward, holding out a hand. She took it, hoping to God it wasn't as clammy as she thought it must be.

She blushed, and he smiled again, the warmth not quite meeting his eyes as he withdrew his hand. "You have business. Care to sit?"

She stepped forward, her heels clicking like gunshots behind him on the hardwood floor of his office. It seemed to take forever to cross the expanse; evidence of how well he'd done for himself.

"Thanks. This is a beautiful office." *Way to go, Katie*, she thought. *Nice sparkling conversation you've got going.*

She took the chair opposite him, put down her portfolio, and crossed her legs. Without thinking, she defensively crossed her arms.

"The perks of being the president," he remarked, closed the open file on the table, and pushed it to one side. Folding his hands in his lap, he wasted no time. "What can I do for you today?"

Ouch. That sounded like a standard line if ever there was one. Looking up at him, she saw his expression was impersonal and barely interested. How could she ever sell him on this idea?

"I'm starting a new business. Unfortunately, financing has been…elusive."

"The banks turned you down." He cut straight to the chase and she winced.

"Yes." Oh, how it hurt to admit it. She'd tried everything, but no one wanted to take a chance on her idea or put the money behind it. She had no experience, few credentials—just a small dream and a desire to make it happen. Apparently the promise to work hard didn't go very far in the business world. She'd done her homework, and though the banks thought her too much of a risk, there was no doubt in her mind she could do this.

"Perhaps you'd better tell me about your venture. I assume it has nothing to do with land development?"

"No, it doesn't. But when I kept hitting brick walls, Dad suggested I try here."

To avoid meeting his eyes, she gazed around his office once more. Being a land developer was his job, and it was obviously very lucrative. Katie smoothed her department store skirt, terribly aware of how circumstances had changed. Richard now held the power to reject her and her idea, and she wondered if he'd turn her down as simple revenge for how she'd treated him in the past. Until now, she'd done a good job of avoiding him. Sucking up to him and his bank balance was something that didn't appeal to her. If only she'd apologized all those years ago, instead of leaving it be. But now their past was like another person in the room with them. She fought to get the words out.

"I want to open a restaurant."

He steepled his fingers and rested them on his lips. "I see."

"Not any restaurant. Something different."

"Everyone thinks their idea is different."

"Y…yes. I'm sure they do," she faltered. She had to convince him that her idea was innovative. And beyond that, profitable. But every time she looked at him, she only saw the hurt in his eyes that day when she'd laughed at him.

He crossed his ankle over his knee, the black trouser leg flawless. "Convince me."

Katie took a breath. Damn him for being completely in control, coolly implacable. She was sure her face was flushed, ruining any effect her careful application of makeup may have had. She uncrossed her arms and reached for her portfolio and the facts and figures she'd brought along to back her up.

"I want to open a healthy choices type restaurant. Nothing upscale, in fact, it would cater mostly to the downtown lunch crowd. All of our selections would be based on sound nutrition. Whole grains, lower in saturated fat, emphasis on vegetables and fruits. An alternative from fast food, if you will, but at the same time a step up. Something to grab on the run, but also to sit down and enjoy."

"Do you seriously think it will fly?"

"Yes, I do," she replied, taking files out of her case. "In fact, I developed a bit of a survey about people's dietary habits, dining out habits, and what sorts of things they'd be interested in. I tabulated the results. It's clear. People are increasingly aware of their health and wanting to eat better, but admit there seem to be few choices for eating out on a budget, and even fewer for eating out without overloading on starch and fats."

She handed him the survey, but continued on as he looked at it, the words spilling out as nervous energy pushed her on.

"Several fast food chains carry salads now. And obviously they're popular, because they haven't pulled them from the market. They're slowly incorporating other healthier choices. It's still a relatively new market, though, and I'd like to get established now. What is it you say? Get in on the bottom floor?"

Richard looked up, met her eyes, and she felt a jolt. He had grown up well. Now he was rich. He'd always said he would be and he'd been laughed at. He'd told her about it one afternoon at a brunch his parents had held. He'd remarked with amazement that she was the first person who hadn't laughed at him.

Now here he was, president of his own company, mature, filled out and handsome. There was more to him than his physical appearance…it was power. It made for a potent combination.

"Katie? I asked if you had a sample menu."

She shook her head, pulled out a sheet and handed it over. "The breakfast menu is small, as you can see."

Ric scanned the menu but Katie continued, amazed he'd even asked to see one. "Egg white omelettes, low fat muffins, multi-grain pancakes, cereals. I'd expect most of the morning traffic to be the coffee crowd, so we'd stock mostly muffins, tea and coffee. Our biggest rush would be at lunch. As you can see, we'd have two hot specials each day…for example, a vegetarian lasagna and perhaps chicken fettuccine in a low fat sauce, or a ratatouille, that sort of thing."

He kept staring at the sheet and her stomach tumbled. Desperate to convince him, she plowed on, "The sandwiches and wraps would be custom-made and served with a side of either one of three salads or a soup. Soup and a whole grain bun will also be a staple of the menu, as well as meal-sized salads. The nice thing about the sandwiches is that they are hot. Grilled chicken and mushroom. Lean steak and peppers. Roasted vegetables, for example. All may be made on a choice of whole grain bread, wraps or pitas. No fried food of any sort. The dessert menu is also small. Fruit cup with dip. Fat free chocolate cake with frozen yogurt. I'm still looking for dessert ideas." She looked up again, surprised his eyes hadn't glazed over.

"And dinner hour? Or does your plan include being closed over dinner?"

"The lunch selections will be available, but in addition we'll have a handful of dinner entrees. Grilled chicken breast, brown rice or baked potato and steamed vegetables; salmon, sole, lean steaks. Marinara sauce with whole wheat pasta. Fajitas. Depending on response we could, and should, adjust the menu accordingly." Katie took a breath as she finished.

He put down the menu and she got the sinking feeling she was going about this all wrong. *Business plan, business plan,* she chanted in her mind.

"Look, menus aside, the most important thing to realize is that there is a real hole in the market for this type of establishment. One of the biggest markets today is weight loss—food, programs, books, you name it. Come out with an eating establishment that carries great tasting food, healthy ingredients and the flexibility to fit it to a specific plan, and you've got a winner."

"And who would do the cooking?"

She paused, expecting some surprise at the least and, most likely, strict resistance. "Me."

"You?"

"Yes. I've worked in the food service industry for several years." She made it sound more than it was and felt a little niggle of guilt over fudging the details.

She should have known he'd persist. He quirked an eyebrow and she felt as if he saw right through that statement. "You've studied?"

"N..no," she stammered. "Not exactly. I've, well, I've worked in several restaurants, either serving or in the kitchen."

He chuckled, leaning back in his chair. "Let me get this straight. You've got no money, no business experience, no chef's diploma to hang on the wall. You've got an idea. That's all. Does that sound like a strong investment to you?"

"Absolutely not," she admitted. "But what I do have is a strong desire to do this and I'm not afraid of hard work. I'm also not scared to learn."

"First of all, tell me why this is important to you." He leaned forward, elbows on his knees, waiting for her answer.

The question threw her. Not once in the meetings she'd held with bankers had they asked that particular question. They had only seen the bottom line—facts and figures. She'd faced the inquisition about work experience, and the answer had always been a resounding no. But Ric wanted to know the why?

"What do you mean?"

"I mean, why now, and why a restaurant? Why this particular kind of restaurant?"

She thought about her answer for a moment before answering. "I've worked in food service for a long time, but one thing always stuck with me. No real thought was put into nutritional content; the ingredients were always full of fat or made with white flour, deep fried or cooked in oil. When Dad had his heart attack, Mom and I started looking at healthier foods.

"You know my dad, Ric. Larger than life and going great guns. Seeing him laying in a hospital bed, frail and grey…it broke my heart. He came home with strict orders for diet and activity. I was still living at home and Mom and I did some experimenting. She lost twenty pounds, and Dad's colour came back. The more I looked into it, I discovered there was a market for fast, healthy, economical food. That's when I realized it was something I could do."

"Do you realize how many entrepreneurs start businesses, only to have them fail in the first two years?"

"Sixty percent. And for the food service industry, it's even higher."

Richard crossed his legs. "And you still want to go through with it?"

"I'll never know unless I try." Looking into his face, she would swear she saw a glimmer of admiration.

"Do you know what causes business to fail? Bad management. Poor marketing. Location. Inadequate financing."

Katie put down the portfolio and started to feel defensive. She wasn't stupid, and she didn't like when people made her feel that way. She knew she could do this. She'd believed him when he'd said he'd be rich one day, and she could make it too.

"I know all that. But I believe in the idea and in myself. I've even found a space to lease. A little tea room off of Third Street. Tell me, Ric, how many people told you you'd fail when you started Emerson Land Development?"

"Plenty." For the first time he smiled. "And I listened to every single one and learned from it."

He rose from his chair and wandered the office for a few moments. Katie forced herself to remain calm and seated. Finally he spoke.

"If I were to finance you, there's still one sticking point for me. You'll never keep customers with poor quality. I think you should reconsider doing the cooking yourself and hire a professional."

"It would be foolish to spend the money on a cook's wages when I can do it myself. I'll already have to hire someone part-time anyway, because I don't plan to be there seven days a week *and* take care of the business end." A thought dawned on her and she ran with it. "I'll make you a deal. You pick a meal from this menu. I'll cook it for you tomorrow night. If you have any doubts about my cooking after that, I'll concede to hiring a chef."

"If you pass, I'll name my terms."

Katie's heart leaped. My God, he was actually considering backing her. All she had to do was cook him a fabulous, healthy meal. She forced herself to sit still while her body vibrated with hope.

He sat back in the blue chair again, retrieved the menu. After a few moments perusing it, he chose. "Chicken fettuccine, with spinach salad and the chocolate cake."

"It's a deal." Hastily she took a note pad out of the portfolio and scribbled down her address. "Here's my address, show up at six. I guarantee you won't regret it, and we can iron out the details over dinner."

Richard looked down at the address. "You're very sure of yourself."

She stood, hoping her wobbly knees weren't obvious. She was glad he thought she was confident, because she felt anything but.

"Yes, I am."

"Then I'll see you tomorrow evening."

He stood and held out his hand, and she was acutely aware of how much he'd grown since high school. Even thought she wore heels, he topped her by a good four inches. For a moment, she panicked. She felt like a teenager again, off-balance and insecure.

There was no way she could wipe her palm on her skirt now, and she hoped it wasn't damp when she clasped his. His fingers closed around hers firmly and her body was electrified by the simple touch.

"Goodbye, Katie."

"Um, yes. Goodbye, Richard."

She withdrew her hand, hurriedly retrieved her case and scuttled out the door, shutting it behind her.

In the elevator, she leaned back against the wall and took several calming breaths. For the first time in several weeks, she felt hope. Hope that she'd actually get this venture off the ground.

Katie smiled widely at her reflection in the mirrored elevator wall. He hadn't said no. Now she was going to cook him a meal that would knock his socks off.

Chapter Two

Katie whisked the sauce viciously, making sure not one molecule of the milk stuck to the bottom of the saucepan. Ten minutes. Ten minutes was all she had left to make sure this was the perfect meal. The water was heating for pasta, the salads were prepared and in the fridge waiting for dressing, the cake was in a domed dish on the counter, and frozen yogurt in the freezer. If everything were under control, why was she such a quivering mass of anxiety? It didn't help that she couldn't stop remembering how he'd looked yesterday or the fact that, as they shook hands, she'd noticed he wasn't wearing a wedding ring. Was there a girlfriend? Someone as rich and good-looking as Ric wouldn't be single for long.

At five to six, the buzzer sounded. Wiping her hands on her apron, she took a breath and pressed the switch for the security system. "Richard?" His name came out trembly with nerves she prayed weren't evident over the scratchy intercom.

"Yes."

She cleared her throat. "Come on up."

She released the button, smoothed her hair, and opened the door when she heard his steps on the stairs. She hoped she looked all right. She'd deliberately chosen a long floral skirt with a black background and a snug black cotton sweater, leaving her arms bare. Over all was a plain white cobbler apron. It had been a tough choice, dressing down or dressing for business. In the end, she'd gone middle of the road. The skirt was flowing and feminine, the colours businesslike, and the fit of the sweater flattering to her figure.

"Come in," she offered politely, and as he filled the doorway, she became acutely aware of how heart-stoppingly gorgeous he'd become. His jaw shone from a fresh shaving, his hair precisely styled with gel. Yesterday he'd been wearing the standard business suit, all dark colours and conservative stripes. But tonight he'd shown up in jeans, casual shoes and a long-sleeved tan T-shirt. She knew clothes. It might be casual but it wasn't bargain basement, and the effect momentarily made her catch her breath.

He stepped inside and looked around the tiny entry. Following his gaze, she realized how very plain her apartment was. By all accounts, Richard was a millionaire. He probably had a fancy house with expensive designer furnishings. Katie, by contrast, had generic beige carpeting, a galley kitchen, a bedroom, office, and a bathroom. The dining room was part of the living room, and the furniture throughout was all second-hand, either cast-offs from her parents or flea markets. It was so unglamorous it wasn't even funny.

"Dinner's almost ready. Make yourself comfortable, I've got a few things to finish up."

Returning to the kitchen, she exhaled as she slid fettuccini noodles into boiling water and continued whisking the sauce. Keeping her hands busy was the only way she was going to keep her tentative grip on control.

Suddenly she realized she hadn't even offered him a drink. Trying to keep things casual, she called into the living room, "Can I get you something cool?"

"Do you have a beer?"

She stirred the pasta gently. "Afraid not. But I have iced tea."

"That'll do," he replied, and she took a pitcher from the fridge. When she turned back, he was standing in the doorway to the kitchen, watching her curiously. The handle of the pitcher grew slick in her hand. He looked entirely too hunky as he filled the small entry to her working space, and she had to remind herself that this was business and not a first date. No matter how much it felt like one.

"Can I help?"

Katie felt her pride pricked. This was her deal, and she had to show him she was capable. Snagging a tall glass from the cupboard, she poured his tea and added a slice of fresh lemon to the top. "No, thanks. It's all under control."

She handed him the glass of iced tea, the ice cubes tinkling. As he took it, their fingers touched, creating a great sense of discomfort borne of awkwardness and attraction. Her insides curled at the brush of his warm hand against hers, and automatically her gaze shot to his. What she saw there was not simple at all…it was magnetic. This was feeling more and more like a first date and not a test and she simply had to ignore the powerful current that arced between them every time they connected.

Which was easier said than done as his gaze delved into hers for a moment and she noticed how extraordinarily long his eyelashes were. The hiss of water boiling over sounded behind her and she jumped.

Hastily grabbing the pot, she put it on a back burner, turning on the heat and turning the front one off. She grabbed the whisk again and stirred frantically, concentrating on the creamy sauce. *Forget bedroom eyes and focus on the task*, she chided herself, becoming annoyed.

"You're distracting me," she complained.

"Sorry," he murmured before disappearing again, the ice rattling in his glass as he retreated.

Oh, for Pete's sake, she thought, placing a hand on her belly to calm the nerves centred there. She was getting all silly over Richard Emerson. The guy who'd actually taped his glasses together in high school. Who'd been a member of the Math Club, the poster boy for anti-acne cream. The nerd who was now a gorgeous millionaire considering backing her business venture. Her stomach began its fluttering again.

She picked up a glass bottle and shook it vigorously, at the same time removing individual salads from the fridge. Taking them to the table, she invited him to sit. He stood, staring out her patio doors at the trees in the back of the building.

"You can start on your salad," she said quietly. "The rest will be out shortly."

"I'll wait for you," he answered.

Without looking at him, she murmured, "Suit yourself. It shouldn't be long."

In the kitchen, she drained the pasta. If he said yes—no, *when* he said yes—to the financing, she'd truly begin with her plans. Renting the space and outfitting it with the equipment she'd require. Decorating it with friendly, welcoming touches. Perhaps some potted plants, cheerful linens. Relaxing, yet generating an optimism. Yes, that was it.

She fixed plates and her plans halted mid-thought. She was getting ahead of herself again. First she had to convince Richard. If things were this strained and awkward, how were they going to get through dinner? They'd have to work out terms, and not for one minute did Katie think Richard would be a push-over. Thankfully, once her financing was in place, the only contact she would have with him would be making repayments on her loan. He had to say yes.

She added fresh parmesan to the sauce, tossed the chicken in with the pasta, and mixed it all together. Scooping servings on to plain plates, she served him, then took her own seat.

He swirled pasta on his fork, tasted. She perched on the edge of her chair, waiting for his verdict, wondering if she'd forgotten anything in the sauce, or if the pasta was too well done…

"It's good."

She hid all her relief and confidently replied, "Of course."

Chewing, he laughed a little. "Don't give me that affronted stare. You look like you're about to suck your lips into the back of your head."

She huffed, realizing her lips had been pursed tightly. "I can cook. Of that I'm sure."

He took another bite and she watched in amazement as he closed his eyes as he chewed. Her gaze was drawn to the motion of his jaw and how strong and sure it seemed.

Swallowing, he took a sip of his iced tea and she stared at his Adam's apple bobbing.

"What makes this healthier than what I'm going to get in the average eatery?"

Relieved he'd kept the topic to business, she attempted a smile. "Well, for starters, the pasta is whole wheat. You've got lean, skinless chicken for protein and the sauce is made from all reduced fat or fat free dairy products."

"I'd expect it to be thinner, less rich."

"Secret ingredient." She smiled then, a little more relaxed. Leaning back in her chair, she let waves of relief guide her away from her building attraction and back to the task at hand. "I could tell you but I'd have to kill you."

He chuckled again and picked up the bottle of salad dressing, giving it a little shake and pulling out the stopper. "And this is homemade too?"

"Yes. Olive oil, red wine vinegar, garlic, a few herbs."

He poured it on his greens and speared a spinach leaf and white mushroom. She relaxed further. She had full confidence in her dressing. It would stand on its own anywhere, and she wasn't surprised when he admitted, "Delicious."

"The salads we'll make up fresh midmorning, and I won't make all my own dressings. Some we'll buy, lower fat or fat free versions, of course. The fettuccine is one example of our hot selection available daily. I've tried it with multigrain pasta, but didn't like it quite as much."

"Hmm," he murmured, and helped himself to a tender piece of chicken. For a moment he was quiet, but his hand traced a pattern on the oak finish of the table. "I recognize this, don't I? Didn't it used to be in your mom's kitchen?"

Oh dear, he'd recognized it. How many other pieces of her furniture would he remember? The sofa? Perhaps the cherry end tables that didn't seem to match? Would he think she was pathetic, unable to provide her own furniture for herself? She refused to meet his eyes as something akin to shame washed through her. So much for success. She wasn't one, and he was—in spades. Ten years ago she'd considered herself superior, but they had certainly reversed positions.

"Um, yeah. When she redecorated, she gave it to me."

When she braved a look up, he smiled gently, devoid of censure. He sensed her discomfort, she was certain. Yet his only response was kind and put her at ease, deliberately, she thought. It was more magnanimous than she'd expected, considering how she'd treated him in the past.

"I always liked this set," he remarked. "Aren't you going to eat?" He gestured towards her plate with his fork.

She laughed, the sound breathy. "I don't know if I can. I'm too nervous."

"Eat. We'll discuss figures later."

"Really?"

He chuckled at her incredulous tone. "Really. As long as dessert is as good as the entrée, we can work something out."

She scooped up pasta, grinning from ear to ear. Oh, wow. This was actually going to happen! When everyone had said nay, Richard was saying yes. He would finance it, take a chance on her. Everything she'd worked for, wanted, was going to become reality. The notion was dizzying!

On the back of her elation came heavy, crippling fear. Now that opening her restaurant was becoming a real possibility, she felt fear of failure overwhelm her in sweeping waves. The Alfredo curdled in her mouth; she put down her fork.

"Are you okay?" Concerned, Richard put down his own fork and leaned over, worry clouding his eyes. "Katie? What is it?"

Pushing her plate aside, she lowered her forehead on to her hands, trying to regulate her shallow breathing. "I'm sorry," she mumbled. "It's just…I don't know…oh, this is ridiculous."

"It's terrifying, isn't it?"

She took three deep calming breaths and looked up. His face had softened and his understanding eyes seemed to invite her to talk. She folded her napkin in triangles over and over again as she admitted,

"Oh Richard, it is. After months and months of being turned away, knowing that it's real...I don't want to screw this up. Oh, that's the wrong thing to say to your investor, isn't it?" Chagrined, she lowered her head again. "I'm such an idiot."

To her surprise, he laughed, and the sound sent warm, calming waves over her.

"First of all, you're not an idiot; don't say that."

That was a surprising boon to her confidence. Considering the reaction she'd been receiving from several corners lately, it almost made her want to cry to have someone believe in her.

"It's a perfectly natural reaction," he continued. "I know exactly what you mean. I made my first land deal and spent twenty minutes in the bathroom throwing up. Don't sweat it."

She lowered her hands and stared. "You did what?"

"It made me completely sick to my stomach." He reached over and laid a reassuring hand on her arm, and she felt the tingles clear up to her shoulder. "It's okay, Katie. What scares you most?" He invited her to confide with a small smile of reassurance.

"Business," she replied, not missing a beat. She envisioned a desk piled with papers needing signatures. She could easily imagine forgetting something and then being without ingredients or permits or worse, getting shut down. Panic churned through her again. "Permits, suppliers, insurance, accounting. I just scraped by in accounting in high school."

"I never knew you took any business courses." He continued eating and it relaxed her, knowing he was carrying on normally.

She sipped her iced tea cautiously found her stomach agreed it was okay. "I took typing, a few other courses. I knew I wasn't college material."

His eyes narrowed curiously. "What makes you say that?"

"I was never smart enough."

He nodded, and she was a little hurt he didn't contradict her.

"Anyway, it's all the legalities that have me frightened. If I could simply snap my fingers and have everything set up, ready to walk into, I'd be happy."

He pushed back his plate and she was surprised to see it empty. She'd hardly tasted her own, but that was all right. She'd eat later, once she settled down.

"I'll get your dessert," she said, rising from her chair.

"It can wait until you eat," he offered politely.

"I'll eat later. When I regain my equilibrium." She disappeared into the kitchen.

She returned with a generous helping of chocolate cake and vanilla frozen yogurt. "Did you want coffee or tea? I have both."

"How about coffee, but in a while? We've got a lot of ground to cover. I have a proposition for you." He dug into the cake, tried a morsel and closed his eyes. "Wow."

"It's fat free."

"You're kidding."

"Not an egg or speck of margarine in sight."

"It's fantastic." He scooped up more, complete with yogurt.

She forced herself to sit still. A proposition? What on earth did he mean? She was sitting on tenterhooks here and he was infuriatingly slow, calmly eating chocolate cake as if her future weren't in the balance. Her knee began to bob impatiently under the table and she began folding squares with the napkin this time.

She forced herself to drink some iced tea. When she couldn't stand it anymore, she prodded, "What sort of proposition do you have in mind, Richard?"

He made her wait until he finished his cake, and she wondered if he'd lick every smear of chocolate and vanilla clean before continuing on. It was maddening. In fact, his whole systematic, orderly calm was maddening. She wanted to charge in and get going!

"First of all," he said, "Call me Ric. You used to in high school and my friends do now."

That almost sounded like a backward invitation to friendship. What she wanted was business backing so she could move forward. Friends were nice to have, but friends with Ric? She wasn't sure that was a good idea. For one, it probably wasn't a good idea to be "friends" with someone who was willing to lend you thousands of dollars. Business and pleasure made for bad bedfellows, a fact of which she was already painfully aware. She wasn't sure being friends was a very good idea in any case. The way Ric looked now—the confidence he showed, his intelligence—she would be in serious danger of developing a crush. And that wouldn't be good for either one of them.

But the fact that he'd equated her to a friend, despite how she'd humiliated him in the past, gently touched her.

"Okay, Ric," she amended, her voice softer than she'd intended. She cleared her throat. "And second of all?"

"Put on the coffee."

She looked into his eyes. They were dark, dark brown and intelligent. They always had been. But never before had she been drawn to them like she was now. He gazed back at her evenly, and she knew instinctively that whatever was coming she wasn't going to find pleasant and he was using coffee as a distraction. Her eyes dropped to his lips and she found that by simply sitting there, he was already distracting her plenty.

"Regular or decaf?" she whispered, and to her embarrassment, he grinned. It was like someone flicked on a halogen lamp, flooding the room with light.

"Regular's fine," he answered, and she hurried to the kitchen again to make it.

She poured the water into the coffee maker, her mind whirling. It was all happening so fast, which seemed strange considering she'd been working towards it for months. The fact that Ric was willing to loan her the money to start up the restaurant seemed too good to be true. And the fact that he'd turned from an ugly duckling into a definitive, if dark, swan made her heart thunder ridiculously. She'd be in terrible danger of developing a serious crush if she weren't careful. She wasn't about to go there again. As the coffeemaker sputtered and spit the brew into the carafe, she filled a sugar bowl and milk pitcher. As she turned the corner to place it on the table, she stopped cold.

Ric leaned over the table, stacking dishes. He placed his beneath hers, tidying, and his jeans stretched taut over a nicely filled out backside. The jeans obviously weren't new, she realized, because her gaze was instantly drawn to a worn rectangle on the right cheek where his wallet lay.

Just when she determined to keep things cool and businesslike, something else about him jumped up and made her take notice. Her mouth went dry and she stood dumb as he turned around and caught her staring.

The dishes sat in his hands, but his cheeks flushed brilliant red.

She broke the silence awkwardly. "Um, cream and sugar." Putting them down, she took the dishes from his hands. "Thanks. I'll bring your coffee in a minute."

Putting the dishes on the counter, she pressed her palms to her face. Hot. For pity's sake, this was getting downright silly. Her hands began to sweat as she took thick blue mugs from the cupboard. This was a business dinner. She had to quit acting like a schoolgirl, blushing and stammering. Wiping her hands on her skirt, she poured the coffee into the mugs and returned to the living room.

Ric sat on the sofa, an ankle crossed over a knee. She winced inwardly; he was sitting on the right side, which was the one with the wonky spring. If it weren't sticking in his butt right now, she'd be a monkey's uncle. But he said nothing as she handed him the mug. He'd moved the cream and sugar to the oak veneer coffee table and, showing a level of comfort she envied, picked up a spoon and fixed his brew the way he preferred.

She followed his lead, sat back on the opposite side of the couch, and silence fell, full and awkward.

After a few minutes that seemed to Katie to take forever, he spoke.

"About my proposition," he began, and Katie half turned so she could see his face.

"I'll put up the money for start-up. Rent, equipment, supplies, permits, whatever's required."

"What are you terms?" Thankfully, interest rates at the moment were reasonable and Katie sucked in a breath. "How about prime plus one percent?"

"That's not acceptable."

Katie put down her coffee and folded her hands in her lap. She'd lowballed him on purpose. "Okay. What's your idea of a fair repayment plan?"

He took a nonchalant sip, and countered, "No repayment plan."

"I beg your pardon?" He couldn't possibly mean he was giving her the money. Thousands of dollars. People didn't just give that away. Confused, she lifted her chin and saw his lips set grimly.

"What I'm proposing, Katie, is a partnership."

Chapter Three

Her heart fell. No, no, no! This was not what she wanted. Turning away, she remarkably kept a tight rein on her emotions. The control of the business must remain with her, and she had to keep her distance from Ric as well. He was too alluring by far. Commanding her iciest tone, she replied, "I'm sorry, but those terms are not acceptable to me."

"What?"

His mug hit the table and she winced.

"Katie, be reasonable. You've never run a business before. I can help. I can deal with all those pesky business chores you're worried about. I can take care of those things so you can run the restaurant."

She rose from the sofa and paced to the balcony doors. She looked out, tears of frustration burning against her eyelids, further fuelling her anger. Why, oh why, would no one believe she could do this? Not only the bankers, but her own family merely smiled indulgently at her. Even her dad had reluctantly said, "If you're not ready to give up on this yet, go see Richard Emerson. He might just be crazy enough to back you."

They meant well, she was sure. But faith in her? None. She blinked back the tears and steeled her backbone. She could not show Ric how emotional she was; it would only serve to reinforce the opinion he must have of her…a dilettante. He hadn't seen her for ten years. How was he to know she'd changed? It was up to her to show him.

"If I wanted to be a restaurant manager, I'd get a job as one. No deal."

He sighed, holding out his hands as she turned to face him. "You're not looking at this rationally. I know about starting a business. I can save you a lot of headache."

And what exactly would that prove? Katie sighed. She needed to show everyone, hell, show even herself, that she was a grown up. She could stand on her own two feet. She didn't want to go through life holding someone's hand for safety.

"Maybe I don't want to be saved. Did you think of that?" She stepped towards him and all her control dissolved as she stared into his incredulous face. "I didn't come to your office looking for a business partner. I came looking for a loan. One I intend to repay on reasonable terms. Not this!" Her arm swept wide in a curt gesture.

His brow furrowed with confusion. "Why not? I don't understand. I thought you'd be a little resistant, but Katie, you're downright hostile. It's a good offer. A beneficial one."

His voice was calmly rational and it only served to infuriate her more. Of course he would think she couldn't do it on her own. That seemed to be the general consensus among her family and friends. She swept a hand over her hair in exasperation. She couldn't blame them; sometimes she felt that way herself.

She'd look in the mirror and still see the girl labeled "The Girl Most Likely to…Have Fun". She'd been given that distinction in twelfth grade and it had stuck. General consensus in the halls was that she wasn't smart enough for greatness, but if you wanted a good time, if you wanted to kick back and relax without worrying about the future, Katie was your girl.

She'd earned the label, she admitted. She'd been a bit of a party girl, more concerned with clothes and hair and boys than studying. But she'd outgrown it. For the few years after high school, her lack of direction had kept her in dead end jobs with no bright prospects for the future. It wasn't long before she realized the good times hadn't been worth it. After a couple of years working as a supervisor in a local eatery, she knew how restaurants worked, and not only the service end. She'd watched, and listened, and learned. She stopped partying and bought a computer, using spare time to do research and put together a business plan. This was how she wanted to redeem herself, but it seemed like everywhere she turned, roadblocks popped up. And she was getting damned tired of taking detours. She had realized something surprising during the initial concept and planning of the restaurant. She was smart. And she was stronger than most gave her credit for.

Each time a roadblock had been thrown in her way, she'd found a way around it. Now, when it was so close she could see the open sign, Ric threw up the one block she wasn't sure she could outmaneuver. She had to do this on her own. It was the only way to validate herself.

No one else seemed to realize it, though, and she could clearly see Ric concurred that this project was beyond her capabilities.

"Why do you want to do this, Ric?" She fisted her hands on her hips. "I mean, you have your own business now. What could possibly entice you to go into partnership with me? You remember what it said under my yearbook picture, don't you? Most Likely to Have Fun?"

She remembered the look of hurt betrayal she'd seen on his face when she'd turned him down for the prom. She'd actually said "You can't be serious!" to him. Immediately she'd regretted the words, but the "girls" had been standing not ten feet away, listening to every word. If she hadn't forgotten that terrible moment, he hadn't either. He sat rigidly on the sofa, saying nothing and it only added to her vitriol.

Frustration bubbled out as she implored him with her hands. "What is it? You want to show me how superior you are now? A little revenge for previous humiliations?"

His mouth fell open and a line of guilt snuck along her spine, but she was too caught up in her own emotions to stop. "You're not alone in thinking I can't do this. Apparently everyone on the face of the planet agrees with you."

"I never said that." He stood now too, and faced her. His lips pressed together, a thin line of annoyance. His shoulders were stiff and his hands rested on his hips. "You haven't even heard me out. This isn't personal. It makes good business sense."

Now, apparently, she didn't have business sense either. "I've heard enough." She squared off against him, feeling small next to his six-foot frame. The little voice in her head that said she wasn't good enough for anything more was now shouting. No one, not even her own family, believed in her. They patted her on the head and loved her dearly, but didn't believe her when she said she could take this dream and run with it; make it a reality.

"This restaurant will be mine, and mine alone. I'll do the work and I'll damn well take the credit. Whoever is smart enough to back me will get their money back along with a reasonable rate of interest for their trouble. But I will not hand the reins over to someone who thinks they know better than I do." She caught her breath, lowering her tone. "Now, if you're done, I'll ask you to leave."

Her stomach lurched as she heard the words come out of her mouth, much stronger than she felt them. She was letting the one chance she had, go. But the last thing she wanted was a partner taking over, which was exactly what would happen. And he'd be around a lot. Too much. Before they knew it, he'd be running everything and she'd be following, rather than leading.

And she knew herself well enough to know that to put Ric Emerson in close proximity for any length of time, she'd screw that up too. She'd let it become personal and lose her perspective—something she couldn't afford to do. She'd hurt him once before, and wouldn't do it again.

His face dropped into a mask of incredulity and he stepped back, shoving his hands into his pockets. "You're kicking me out?"

"You bet your sweet chequebook."

Two distinct lines of disapproval wrinkled between his brows as quiet settled, heavy and uncomfortable. "I see," he said quietly. "Well, good luck finding a backer, Katie. You're going to need it."

She didn't miss the arrogant note in his voice. As she shut the door behind him, she had the sinking feeling she'd just ruined everything.

She sank to the couch, her head in her hands. She'd let her temper get the better of her again, but she was so…frustrated! Tears stung her eyes again. She should have known it was a mistake to go to Richard Emerson for help. She should have foreseen he'd be changed. She should have been prepared for attraction, especially after all the undercurrents that had shimmered between them yesterday. She should have been armed with a better argument against partnership.

Instead she'd lost her cool and had sent him and his money packing. Would she ever learn how to handle him? And could she possibly find a way to salvage everything?

ℬ ℭ

She'd be back.

He'd give her three days. Three days and she'd be knocking at his office door, asking him to reconsider lending her the money. Even now, he bet she was going through the tortures of hell, wondering how she could get the business off the ground now that her best chance had walked out the door. Still, the evening hadn't been a waste. Not at all. He'd had a delicious meal and seeing Katie all fired up with righteous indignation…his eyes crinkled at the corners as he laughed a little. Her blue eyes shot fire and her cheeks turned the most adorable shade of pink. It would almost be worth getting her angry more often, to see those sparks. She was more beautiful now than she'd been at seventeen. Her hair was the same honey blonde, but she'd gone from cheerleader-cute to beautiful in the intervening years. Her body was curved in all the right places, he thought, as he recalled the fitted suit she'd worn yesterday. And she'd learned a thing or two about makeup application.

Turning the key in the lock, Ric stepped into his northwest home and pressed his security code into the alarm system. With a plaintive "meow", Gilligan emerged from the den and curled his fluffy black tail around Ric's legs. "Hey, boy," he crooned, stroking his hand down the cat's silky fur. "Hungry?"

The cat meowed again. Ric headed for the kitchen first and filled Gilligan's bowl with cat food. The sound of the cat eating echoed through the large kitchen and Ric felt, as he frequently did, lonely. Most people thought Gilligan's name cute and funny. Only Ric knew he'd named the cat that because he felt, most of the time, like he was alone on an island.

This house was simply too big for a bachelor, but he'd loved it the moment he saw it anyway. Situated on the northwest edge of Calgary, he had a mountain view and twenty-five hundred square feet to himself. Warm mornings, he had his coffee on the deck and watched deer and rabbits forage for food. Cool evenings, he put on a fire in the gas fireplace and worked on whatever he'd brought home from the office.

But much of the time, he seemed to rattle about in it himself. He'd only been here a week when he'd gone to the SPCA to get a companion. Dogs were too fussy. He wanted a pet with attitude and independence. Gilligan had stared at him through the cage, then turned away as if saying, "Adopt me or don't. Whatever." He had, and at least someone was waiting at home for him now.

He took a beer from the fridge, popped the top, and headed out to the deck.

Katie'd hardly changed since high school, he thought, shaking his head and taking a long drink. Her smile was still magnetic and her voice hadn't changed at all. Her refusal of him tonight definitely held echoes of that day ten years ago.

He leaned against the wooden railing and gazed at the sun sliding below the mountains, shadowing the soft remnants of snow barely covering the bowls and peaks. He sighed. He hadn't been good enough for her then. And she'd clearly told him he wasn't good enough now. The thought of working with him had caused such a violent reaction in her he couldn't help being offended. He'd changed, made sure of it. He'd used his brains and determination to transform his body and build a successful company. In his heart he knew a large part of it had been wanting to show her what she'd turned away. The fact she didn't seem any more interested now than she had then made him wonder why he'd done it at all. And yet…he couldn't be sorry. Even without her, he was proud and happy with the changes he'd made to his life.

He took another long drink of the locally made brew. He still heard her voice, all those years ago. *"You can't be serious,"* she'd said, and before she even laughed, he'd heard the snickers of her girlfriends around the corner of the locker. After the brunch the weekend before, he'd thought he'd stood a chance, but she'd cleared that little misconception up in a hurry. The way she'd looked down her nose at him…he'd felt angry, not with her but with himself, hating his skinny arms and legs and the cowlick that permanently marred his hair. He hated his thick glasses and button down shirts. In that moment, he'd never felt lower, and he had spent four years rebuilding himself, vowing never to give anyone that power again.

Then, yesterday, she'd shown up at his office and he'd been absurdly pleased she could see for herself that he'd become the success he'd vowed he would. He'd felt momentarily proud of what he'd achieved, yet left wanting something more. He wanted Katie to see him for who he was. Not the boy he'd been and the man he'd become, but why and how he'd done it.

Looking down over the yard and into the gulley below, he watched a coyote skim stealthily through the grass. She'd come to him asking for money. The land development business wasn't as exciting as it had once been and he needed a change. He thought perhaps working together would be fun, now that they'd grown up. It would give him a chance to show her who Ric Emerson truly was.

But clearly she wasn't interested in that. He gave a derisive snort, aimed more at himself than anyone else. He'd deluded himself into thinking she'd be happy at the chance. How silly. She wanted his money. That was all, and the truth of it stung.

But her business plan was good sense so he'd give her the money at a reasonable rate of interest. The girl who had listened to his dreams in math class and who had been nice to him at family functions deserved that much. She'd sat with him at brunches and dinners and hadn't acted like it was a chore. In senior year, she'd convinced him to enter a young entrepreneur competition, and he'd won an internship at a prestigious land development company. After that summer, he'd known what he'd wanted to do. He wouldn't be where he was today if it hadn't been for her gentle encouragement.

Because he owed her that much, he'd make a few phone calls, make sure she got things going smoothly without knowing he had a hand in it. He had an investment to protect, after all, and if she went bankrupt, he'd be out the money. And it would give him a chance to keep tabs on her anyway, under the guise of a concerned investor. Now that they'd made contact again, he wasn't prepared to just let her disappear as she once had.

His cell phone vibrated against his side, and he checked the number. He answered and, cradling the phone against his ear, went back inside to make the deal, closing the sliding doors behind him.

೫೦ ೦೩

She only took two days, and for the second time in a week, Katie stood nervously in his office.

He looked down at her. She'd worn slacks today, black ones, with black, strappy, three-inch heels that made her legs look long and slim. Her toenails were painted a pretty soft pink. Her hands were unadorned, but she wore a dainty pink and silver bracelet on her right arm, the colour matching her soft sweater perfectly. To anyone else she was dressed appropriately, but Ric was stunned by her femininity, her simple beauty.

He wished he could disassociate that part of her from business, but he couldn't. He'd always had a thing for Katie, even when she'd rejected him publicly. The sick feeling returned to the pit of his stomach, an automatic response when he felt a failure. He willed it away, focusing on the reason for their meeting. He'd rather forget about that day altogether and get on with things. With the future.

He preferred to leave the emotional outburst from the other night in the past. It wouldn't serve either one of them to get wound up now. It would only breed more misunderstandings and hurt feelings. This had to stay all about business as far as Ric was concerned.

"Have a seat," he offered with a small, intimate smile. "Would you like some coffee? Tea?"

She slid into the blue chair and put her purse beside it, her eyes watching him nervously as if trying to figure out what he was thinking. "Coffee, I guess. Milk and sugar."

He called out to his assistant and shuffled over the papers on his desk until he found the file he was looking for. The assistant brought in a plain tray carrying two cups of coffee and placed it on the table between the blue chairs.

"This is very nice," Katie began, her voice shaking a little as the assistant shut the door behind her. "But I'm actually here to…um…"

"Yes?" he prompted, his eyebrows lifted hopefully. It wasn't going to be easy to keep things impersonal. He had papers in his hand, ones about lending her capital. But he found he wanted to hear what she had to say first. He picked up his mug and took a long sip, shuttering away any feelings, hiding any hope he had that she might change her mind.

She sighed, loudly, turning her mug around and around in her hands. "Oh dammit, Ric, I came to grovel. To tell you I'm sorry for jumping all over you the other night. I have no excuse for my behaviour. I've reconsidered your offer." The words came out in a rush, like she wanted to get it over with.

Very quietly, his back to her, he put the file back on the desk and closed his eyes with relief. She was working her way up to signing the deal, and inexplicably his heart leapt. The urge to keep her close, not to lose touch again was strong, but he was certain that if she knew the direction of his thoughts, she'd run completely in the other direction. Opening his eyes, he found himself staring at a tiny gold toe ring on her right foot. It was a very pretty toe, precisely painted with a tiny pink jewel set in the middle.

In many ways she hadn't changed since high school, and she'd made his pulse jump. Her favourite colour had been pink back then too, and she'd painted her toes in chemistry class senior year, making him roll his eyes. Her resulting low laugh had affected him in every way expected of a seventeen-year-old boy. She still held that power, with no more than a toe jewel.

He swallowed, turned, and answered, "I'm glad."

"You are?"

He smiled, genuinely. "I didn't like how we left things."

She crossed her legs and picked up her coffee, then put it down again. "Me either." Folding her hands together, she twisted her fingers. Ric noticed, touched she was nervous. He thought perhaps she was feeling now as he had, when he'd asked her to the prom. Vulnerable and anxious.

"Um…is the offer still open?"

"Are you sure you want it to be?"

"I'd be willing to discuss the possibility of a partnership with you," she said, her voice clear but with a slight wobble. "I hope I didn't burn any bridges the other night."

His tone was strong and carried a bit of censure as he replied. "You kicked me and my chequebook out, as I recall."

He wasn't letting her off easily.

"I know. I'm afraid I feel very strongly about this. I let my emotions get the better of me and…and that was wrong."

He sat in the chair opposite her. "You've reconsidered."

"Y…yes, if it's not too late," she answered, her fingers twisting again.

"And you're willing to have me as a business partner."

After a pause, her words came clearly. "Business, yes."

His gaze met hers sharply. Well. That was definitive. Business only. He should be relieved, he supposed.

"You've been very honest about this being only about the money."

To his surprise, she dropped her eyes and blushed again.

"It's nothing to be ashamed of," he continued, his voice matter-of-fact. "It'll make working together much easier than having a lot of atmosphere between us."

When she looked up again, he kept his expression completely neutral. Her face, however, was a contradiction. Her lips were firm and decisive, yet her eyes were evasive, not quite meeting his and her cheeks held a flush that suggested some internal discomfort. Patiently, he waited for what she wanted to say.

"I want you to understand about something, Ric. That day when you asked me to the prom, I…"

He lifted a hand, silencing her. This wasn't what he expected, nor what he wanted to talk about. "It was ten years ago, Katie. We don't have to discuss it."

Her chin flattened at his abrupt interruption. "Are you sure?"

Oh yeah, he was sure. Really sure he didn't want to dredge up embarrassments and hurt feelings that happened a decade in the past. He'd worked very hard to change his image to look like the successful, confident businessman. And for the most part, it worked. But inside he was still a math geek who had once thought he might have a chance with Katie Buick. He wasn't going to put himself out there again.

"Yeah, I'm sure."

A long pause filled the room.

"Then why, Ric? Why do you want to be a partner if it doesn't have anything to do with me?"

He crossed his ankles, ran a finger over his bottom lip. "You see this office? This is my kingdom." His smile was half-hearted and a little cold. "I love what I've built, but sometimes I feel…trapped? Like I need a change. Something different to inspire me. A new project to sink my teeth into."

"I'm surprised."

"Even millionaires get bored."

She smiled at that. "I wouldn't know," she replied warmly, and they both relaxed considerably.

"You know about how a restaurant works. I know about business. We can each play to our strengths and it'll stand a much better chance of success."

"Which guarantees your investment."

"Precisely."

"But I need to learn about the business part too. I don't want to have to rely on you. No offense."

"None taken." He sank back into his chair. "It would definitely be better if you learned the ropes. I do have an empire to run."

She snorted, let out a little giggle. "My, my. A sense of humour. I'd forgotten about that."

Smiling at each other, he felt connected in a way he hadn't for a long time.

"All right. Will you teach me, Ric?"

"More than you'll ever want to know," he answered, meaning spreadsheets and forms and red tape, but once the words were out of his mouth, he felt the attraction he'd always felt for her simmering beneath again.

"It's very overwhelming." Her voice carried a note of worry that touched him, and against his better judgment, he went to her chair and knelt beside it.

"You have your hair down," he murmured, his gaze roving over the golden strands.

She blushed, and he did too, and suddenly it was like the restaurant idea faded into background as she stared into his face. All he could see was the golden mass falling on her shoulders, and all he wanted was to do what he hadn't for ten long years.

Cautiously he lifted his hand, but paused inches away from her hair. His dark eyes met hers, blue and wide with shock, and he fought the terrible urge to lean in the few inches and kiss her to make the memory complete.

Oh my God.

Katie's breath caught in her throat as Ric knelt beside her. She looked up at him, her eyes widened with awareness and surprise as she saw desire in his. He'd been cool, collected until now, but suddenly she was shockingly aware that he was indeed attracted to her. If they kept staring at each other like love-struck fools, she knew absolutely that he would lean in and kiss her.

Like she wanted him to. Her fingers stopped twisting and she had the brief fantasy of leaning in and sinking her fingers into the dark curls at the nape of his neck.

"What are you doing?" she demanded, blinking and pulling back in her chair.

He withdrew without touching her; he cleared his throat and rose.

Her lungs filled with air again as he moved to maintain a better distance. How could she work with someone she found herself undeniably attracted to?

"Maybe this isn't such a good idea," she whispered, half to herself, grabbing for her purse. She thought of the restaurant and halted.

She put her purse back down and heard him exhale, slowly.

"It won't happen again." Something in his tone told her he was deeply offended, yet explanations were useless right now.

He could not know how close she'd come to touching him, to wondering what his lips would feel like on hers…

She would have to simply ignore that. There could be no more deep gazes and thoughts of kissing.

Katie stood. "Then I'll come armed with facts and figures next time."

"And I'll have papers drawn up. Does Monday morning work for you?" He stood too. Their meeting was obviously concluding.

"Ten o'clock?"

"Sounds good."

She held out her hand. "See you then, partner."

Ric took her hand in his and felt the jolt clear to his gut. He looked down into her eyes as their fingers clung longer than necessary.

"Partner," he replied.

After she was gone, the scent of her perfume lingered and he wondered how the hell he was going to work with her day in and day out without completely going crazy.

Chapter Four

Monday morning at nine fifty-five, Katie stepped inside a downtown coffee shop, jittery with excitement. This was going to happen. With Ric's help, her dream was coming true.

She checked the specials on the board but, pressing a hand to her stomach, knew she couldn't eat. Ric had called and left a message on her machine about meeting here instead of at ELDC, and she was glad. She felt incredibly intimidated in his office, both by the size and the importance it seemed to exude. She scanned the informal seating area, and noting Ric hadn't arrived yet, she escaped to the ladies room to check her appearance. Under the fluorescent light, she gave her hair one last pat. She'd put it up in an intricate twist, her makeup was carefully applied, and she wore a new outfit—a black and cream linen dress. She was completely put together. In her purse was the pen her grandmother had given her for graduation. She thought it appropriate to sign the papers with it.

Somewhat satisfied with at least her outward appearance, she stepped out and found an empty table in the corner.

After today, everything would change. She and Ric would be partners. She'd be committed to a new business. After today, she'd be a grownup. The thought was both exhilarating and daunting.

Ric swung through the door a moment later. Her heart thumped traitorously in response to his GQ appearance. She'd never gone for the suit and tie type, but Ric looked at home, very right in them.

"Good morning, Katie," Ric said, putting his briefcase down by the vacant chair. "You ready?"

His eyes were like warm chocolate and she noticed his tie was a little off centre. "As ready as I'm going to be." She smiled in response, waving out her hand, offering him to sit.

As he put his briefcase on the table and opened it, she caught the sparkle of a ring on his right pinky. His graduation ring, she supposed, from when he'd done his MBA. She tried to ignore the reminder that he was far better educated than she. The last thing she needed to do was dig out a yardstick and start making comparisons.

The comforting odour of coffee was thick in the air. "It's a big day today," he smiled at her. "For both of us."

She took a deep breath. "You're an old hand at this stuff," she chided. "I'm a newbie. I've been a bundle of nerves all morning."

"That's where you're wrong." He closed the case again and put it back on the floor beside his feet. "I'm very excited about this. I didn't realize how much I needed a new project. Putting this together is going to be a challenge—and fun.

"I've had papers drawn up. It states the amount I'm investing and delineates my role, as well as percentage of profits. You can take them with you today, have a lawyer look them over, and bring them back when they're signed."

"Oh. I thought I'd just sign them and be done with it."

His smile was indulgent and she knew right away she'd made her first mistake.

His fingers toyed with a pen. "I can go over them with you, of course, but you really should have a lawyer look at them before you sign anything."

"I trust you not to cheat me, Ric."

The pen stopped moving and his eyes warmed. "I'm glad. Partners should trust each other."

She picked up the sheaf of papers and scanned them briefly, picking out the main points. She stopped when she reached the section about profits. He'd indicated a sixty-five/thirty-five split. In her favour. It was more than she'd expected and she hoped he wasn't being lenient because of who she was. She wasn't sure what to say.

"You've given me sixty-five percent of the profits."

"Too little?"

"I thought as partners, we'd split them equally. I don't want any special treatment." She had tried to make it clear she wanted to be treated as he'd treat any partner.

"You won't get any. I have ELDC to run as well; you'll be putting more hours in at the restaurant than I will. This is your baby. I thought it only fair you get a higher percentage."

"Thank you." The rest of the document seemed to be filled with legalese. He was right; she should go over this with a lawyer. "I'll have them back to you before the end of the week," she suggested, and he nodded.

A heavy pause fell between them and Katie resisted the urge to shift in her seat. Business was concluded yet Katie didn't feel like leaving yet, and Ric didn't seem to be in much of a hurry either. He cleared his throat and she looked up expectantly.

"Have you had breakfast?" he asked. "I'm in the mood for coffee and bagels."

49

Breakfast? Hardly. She hadn't been able to eat a bite this morning in all her nerves and preparation. "No, I haven't eaten," she replied.

"I have some time," he continued, and stood, smiling down at her. "We can talk about our ideas for the restaurant."

She put the contract in the brown envelope he provided. "That sounds good."

He went to the counter and ordered two cinnamon raisin bagels and two large coffees. Steam curled off the paper cups and mingled with the scent of cinnamon and raisins.

"Okay," he began easily, "what should we tackle first?"

Katie bit into her bagel, licking a spot of cream cheese from the corner of her mouth. It was silly, but she felt self-conscious simply eating in front of him. He always seemed put together, and sharing breakfast took on an intimacy that was surprising. She made sure she swallowed the entire mouthful before replying.

"Well, I suppose we should look after renting the space first, making sure of zoning, that sort of thing."

He nodded, took a drink of his coffee and winced. "Ooh, that's hot," he gasped, and Katie laughed, relaxing. Well, perhaps he wasn't quite perfect.

"You mentioned the tea room on Third. I have my reservations about that location."

Katie put down her bagel and wiped her fingers on a paper napkin as intimacy flew right out the window. This was how it would begin, then. The very first issue and they would be at odds, and she could tell he was used to getting his way. Perhaps being a partner wouldn't be such a good idea, if he thought he could strong arm her. At least the papers weren't signed yet.

Or, perhaps she was being over-defensive. She measured her words carefully, keeping all accusation out of her tone.

"You have a problem with the space I've chosen? Why?"

"It's not central enough. Yes, it's downtown, but you want to be somewhere where you'll get volume, and lots of it, especially during the noon hour. I know of a property available…"

She cut him off. "Of course you do."

His mouth closed firmly at the acid in her tone and she uncrossed her legs beneath the table. Now she was feeling patronized. Not only did he not approve of her location, but he had an alternative all lined up. How many other decisions would he take out of her hands?

"What's that supposed to mean?"

"It means, I should have expected you'd disagree with me and…"

"And have a viable alternative? How rude of me." His lips thinned and he put down his coffee.

She blinked. "What I mean is that this was my idea. It's my baby, as you pointed out. I don't want or need you coming in and taking over, remember?"

He pushed his paper plate aside and leaned in on his elbows. "It's my money funding this operation. And guess what? I expect a return on it. Don't forget, Katie, the main objective is to make money, and location is a huge part of that. Your ego has nothing to do with this at all."

"You'll say that every time you want to get your own way."

"No, I'll say that every time my experience tells me what a right decision is."

She shoved back from the table, her pride pricked. "You're insufferable. This was such a mistake." She gathered up her purse.

"Sit down."

Her eyes widened at his imperious tone and she sat.

"Katie Buick, you want to be a grown up, act like one."

"How dare you? You know nothing about me," she spit. "Nothing at all!" Boy, she was getting sick and tired of being accused of immaturity. Trying to overcome her shortcomings was like swimming upstream in a strong current. It didn't matter how hard she tried, she didn't seem to get anywhere and she was getting tired. She wasn't a party girl, at least not anymore. And perhaps she'd been lacking in motivation and ambition. Until she'd found a passion. Once she'd found that, she'd discovered she had both those qualities in abundance.

"I know enough to know you aren't mad about the location. You're all upset because I suggested something different. You want everything your way. Get over yourself, and think of the business first and not your pride."

"Gee, Ric, tell me how you really feel," she muttered, sucking her lips back in from their sulking posture. It only fuelled her anger to know he was right.

Then his lips squirmed as he tried not to smile at her pouting face. She saw a tiny hint of teeth and found herself smiling back despite herself. Suddenly they were laughing and the dark cloud of hostility lifted.

"Look," he said, leaning back in his chair, his eyes crinkling at the corners, "why don't you come and look at the property I'm talking about. If you don't like it, if the kitchen is too small or whatever, I'll concede to look elsewhere. But don't dismiss it out of hand, okay?"

A huge sigh drifted out as she capitulated. "I can probably do that."

"I don't want us to fight every time there's a decision to be made. You need to trust me, Katie."

"And you need to trust me."

"I do. You don't trust yourself. That's why you get defensive, and then you overreact."

She bristled out of habit, but took a deep breath and made herself relax. Strangely enough, she felt safe with Ric, and that was a new feeling.

"I know it. I've spent so long trying to prove myself that I give myself doubts." She played with a ring on the middle finger of her right hand. "I'm terribly afraid you'll just take over. I'm more afraid I'll let you." Her mind flicked back to another memory and she felt the betrayal burn in her stomach. She wouldn't make the mistake of leaving her future in someone else's hands again.

He leaned forward, close enough that as she looked in his eyes she saw tiny gold flecks in the brown surrounding his pupils. Close enough she could have counted his long eyelashes. Her breath caught and she called herself a fool for being easily affected.

"I would never, ever take advantage of you, Katie."

Oh, that took on a whole other meaning when he was so close she could smell his cologne. Being taken advantage of by Ric Emerson was an enticing thought. Who could have guessed he'd grow up to be devastatingly attractive? And it wasn't only his looks. It was his quiet confidence. The way he garnered respect without demanding it.

"I want to believe that," she whispered back, still holding his gaze, and she couldn't help but remember again how she'd hurt him before. "But it's hard."

Her cheeks burned as she heard the words and the implied innuendo she hadn't meant.

"Yes. Well. How about that space? Want to have a look?"

"Now?"

"Bring your coffee."

She stood, capping her cup and grabbing her purse as she trailed after him. "But don't you have to call the leasing company or something?"

He held open the door and as she passed in front of him he said casually, "I've got the key. I own it."

On the sidewalk she spun on him, incredulous. "I should have guessed. You know, you talk out of both sides of your mouth. Out of one you say you don't want to take over, and out of the other you end up owning the most suitable property I could imagine."

He sighed. "Do you always question everyone's intentions?"

"Oh, absolutely. Everyone has an agenda. And I'm not going to be the one to get left behind again."

He raised an eyebrow and took her elbow. "Remind me to ask you about that sometime," he remarked. "There's a story there, I can tell."

"Don't try to humour your way out of this." Her heels clicked frantically as she tried to keep up with Ric's long strides. "Where is this splendid property, anyway?"

"Stephen Avenue."

Her mouth clamped shut. A space on Stephen Avenue didn't come cheaply; in fact, she could never afford the rent on her own. It was a prime location...but why did Ric always have to be right? It was a detail that stuck in her craw and put her on the defensive immediately. Despite the fact they were partners, she was already feeling like someone who was tagging along.

They turned a corner and walked down another block. Ric stopped in front of a building that didn't stand out whatsoever, except for the huge windows in the front. It was flat and brown with dingy beige awnings over the windows. This was it? It was drab and dismal. He put his key in the door and opened it.

A counter in deep red curved around the west wall, the glass over the edge dusty from abandonment. The floors were white speckled industrial tile. She stepped in, running her fingers over the Formica countertop. It definitely had potential—a lot of it. What it needed was a fresh and capable hand to spruce it up and make it fantastic. Already she could see the food lined up behind the counter, smell the fragrance of fresh coffee and baked bread, hear the clicking and beeping of the cash register in the corner. "What used to be in here?" she asked, her voice echoing in the naked space.

"A sandwich shop. Didn't make it though." He was still standing by the door, watching her wander through.

Soberly she removed her hand and wandered towards the back. By the far wall there was a pass-through, and she lifted it, going behind the counter. A sandwich shop—and an economic casualty. Could she ensure that her restaurant wouldn't end up the same way?

"There's an office in the back, and a storage room, naturally."

She looked out over the emptiness, envisioning tables and chairs filled with chatting lunch goers. She saw potted trees in the corners, friendly prints on the walls.

"You're seeing it, aren't you," Ric's voice interrupted quietly.

She met his gaze and knew he was seeing it too. He'd known she'd like it, because he had the same vision. She couldn't hate him for that.

She smiled. "Yes, I'm seeing it."

"The rent comes pretty cheap, considering the location."

She laughed lightly. "You were right, it *is* perfect." She lifted wistful eyes to his. "Promise me something?"

"It depends."

"Let me be right sometimes. I'm going to need that."

"I'm no interior decorator; I'm sure you'll do much better at that than I would."

"Then I guess in addition to the partnership, there's a lease to sign." She held out her hand. "Partner."

"Partner, he echoed, taking her hand over the countertop, and the deal was sealed.

ℰ ℛ

Ric checked his watch for the third time. She was late. He'd postponed a meeting so he could meet Katie for drinks—and to discuss the restaurant. They hadn't been in contact for over a week, and things had to be done.

Besides, he was looking forward to seeing her.

He'd admitted that much to himself. He'd also admitted he was grudgingly gaining respect for her. He admired what she was doing. It took guts to start up a business from the ground up—and with nothing. He was impressed with the amount and quality of her research regarding the market. And judging by the work already underway, he knew she was putting in long, arduous days.

He had risen above his shortcomings and become a success. He admired Katie's work ethic, which was enabling her to do the same. After he'd completed a routine background check on her, he knew exactly what she was trying to overcome, and couldn't help but be impressed by her tenacity.

The door opened and Ric knew before even looking that it was Katie. Something in the air changed; a smell, a charge, he wasn't sure but turning his head he saw she'd arrived, shaking an umbrella and closing it up before scanning the room for him. The moment she saw him, she smiled, and a jolt of electricity shot to his toes.

"Something to drink?" he asked as she took the seat opposite him.

Katie put down her umbrella and ran a hand through her hair. "God, yes. I'm run ragged."

Ric grinned and beckoned for a waitress. "I thought this was better than the office. Sometimes it's good to get out of there. Neutral territory, so to speak."

A waitress with a blonde ponytail and a black apron appeared and Katie smiled. "I'll have a pint of honey-brown," she ordered, and Ric ordered the same.

"I brought some things for you to look at." Ric pulled a file out of his briefcase, wasting no time getting down to business. "First thing we have to do is get our legalities in order."

Their beer arrived and Katie took a long drink. Ric raised one eyebrow as she licked the foam from her top lip, and was rewarded with a laugh.

"I spent the morning looking into equipment suppliers. Let's just say the price tag was, well, shocking." Her eyebrows lifted to emphasize her point.

"I bet."

"I'm thinking secondhand might be the way to go. Either from someone who's going out of business, or I heard about an auction coming up this Thursday. I thought I might go, see if there's anything worth bidding on."

"That sounds smart." Ric sipped his pint, unable to take his eyes off her face. Tiny droplets of water clung to her hair and gave her skin a fresh, dewy glow. "I've got reams of paperwork here, for both of us to sign. I should have anticipated the number of licenses and permits we'd need." He ticked them off on his fingers. "A business license, food establishment license, vendor permit, tax forms, zoning, insurance, the list goes on." He'd been through it before, and it was still daunting.

"God."

"Everyone gets a piece, before we even open."

Katie put down her glass and pulled out a pen. "I'm assuming you've had Dave look everything over? What do I have to sign?"

He smiled then, his eyes crinkling at the corners as he quickly dismissed a prick of jealousy. "You're on a first name basis with the lawyer, now?"

She blushed. "Yeah. Scary, isn't it?"

Dave McDonald was Ric's business attorney and he'd agreed to handle the legalities for the restaurant too. Katie had liked him immediately. He wasn't stuffy or boring. The first time they'd met, he'd been in jeans and a white golf shirt and had just come from his son's rugby game. He was a shade taller than she was, with curly sandy-blonde hair and sparkly blue eyes that screamed mischief. She felt much more comfortable with him, knowing he was relaxed with a real sense of humour. At least she didn't feel intimidated by a stuffed shirt in a three piece suit.

Ric signaled for two more pints and handed over a sheaf of papers. "You can start there. Have a quick look and once everything is in order, I'll file them at City Hall and the tax forms with Revenue Canada. How go the renovations?"

Katie beamed. "I love it. You should come by. The colours are fabulous, and the flooring is perfect." She looked down on the first form. "Um, Ric, we don't have a name for the place yet."

"I thought I'd leave that up to you."

She looked up. "Really?"

"I named my business Emerson Land Development. Doesn't smack of creativity, does it."

"Well…"

"I'm sure you'll come up with something much more zippy and appropriate."

She put down her glass and folded her hands on the table. "I do have an idea, but I'm not sure if you'll like it or not. And I don't want to start another argument."

He shrugged his shoulders. "Ask me." He handed the waitress a bill as she delivered their second drinks.

"How about Pick and Choose?" Before he could say anything, she hurried on to explain her logic. "Customers come in, looking for an alternative, and they get choices. The menu is very flexible, and can pretty much be mixed and matched to satisfy any diet plan out there. They can pick and choose amongst the offerings and get exactly what they want."

"You seem to be in an awful hurry to justify the name to me."

"I…I thought you'd hate it." *On principle, because you didn't think of it,* she thought to herself. Personally she thought it quick and clever, but she'd wanted the tea room space too and now they were setting up shop on Stephen Avenue.

"I think it's brilliant."

"You do?" Her eyebrows lifted. He wasn't going to put up a fight at all?

"I do. You look surprised." He chuckled. "You really need to work on your confidence, Katie. I'll run it through registries and make sure there's not another one listed. If not, I'll register the name, okay?"

"Yeah, okay." She exhaled and started signing beside various x's on the sheets.

"You want company at the auction?" His voice interrupted her progress.

"Naw, I'm fine." Katie didn't look up, just kept skimming and signing. "I've got the chequebook." She grinned out the side of her mouth. "I love spending your money."

"You sound like a wife."

Her hand stilled. It was a joke, she knew it. They'd had none of the tense atmosphere between them today, but with one sentence, she felt the pull to him again. Like there was something more between them, something bigger than both of them, and she didn't want there to be. He was handsome and way too nice, and what she was feeling was surely nothing more than a crush. It would pass, and the best thing to do would be to wait for it to go away rather than act on it.

Besides, she'd made that mistake once before. And she'd learned her lesson after being burned.

"Katie?"

She cleared her throat. "Sorry. I got to thinking for a minute. You can come to the auction if you want."

She felt the coolness between them right away as he responded. "No, that's okay. I probably shouldn't take the time away from work. Why don't you come over on Saturday and pick up your copies of the paperwork? I'll be out of the office on Friday and Monday I'm flying up to Edmonton for a meeting."

"To your house?"

"Is that a problem? There's a lot of work to do, and it's probably the best way to do it uninterrupted. If you don't mind working on a Saturday."

Oh, no, no problem at all. Except he kept making it harder and harder for her to keep her distance. She already had to fight the urge to look. Put them in close proximity too much and before she knew it she'd be touching. Her fingertips tingled at the thought.

Her voice came out more strained than she liked. "Not at all. I'll bring coffee. You keep the pencils sharp."

She looked at her watch; it was already past four. "I've gotta run, I've got dinner plans with Mom and Dad," she made a hurried excuse. "I'll see you Saturday. Thanks for the beer."

She grabbed her bag and hurried to rise.

"Katie? Don't you need the address?"

She flushed and stammered, "Uh, yeah, I guess I do." She was flustered at the thought of spending a day with Ric in such an intimate setting and it was affecting her thinking.

Ric wrote it on a napkin and handed it over. "Saturday, then."

His fingers brushed hers and startled gazes clashed at the contact. His thumb pressed against her fingers as butterflies danced in her stomach.

She pulled away and, instead of answering, simply fled.

Chapter Five

Ric gave a quick check in the mirror, running his fingers through his hair and scowling at a stubborn curl that wouldn't go where he wanted. It was only Katie Buick and they were only doing work. He didn't need to take time to primp and preen.

Only Katie Buick.

He sneered at the reflection in the mirror with self-deprecation. Who was he kidding? He'd done a lot of things in his life in the name of Katie. In high school, he'd tried to get her attention, to show her he was smart and determined. At times, he'd been sure she'd seen past his big glasses and skinny body to the heart inside. But she'd rejected him and from that moment he'd determined he'd make the outside as dynamic as the inside. He may have had intelligence and drive, but he needed to look successful.

His first year of university, he'd approached a sports coach about getting in shape and proper nutrition. It was a regimen he still followed, daily.

In the kitchen, he wiped the counter and put his glass and the top of the blender into the dishwasher, wiping the stainless steel door with a towel. He'd already been up, had his egg white omelette, worked out, and finished with his protein shake. Now, at nearly ten, he was showered and dressed.

The doorbell rang, shaking him out of his thoughts with a start. *Forget about it being Katie, and stick to business,* he reminded himself, walking to the door.

For some reason, he wanted her to approve—of him, of his business, of his house. He didn't want to be seen as lacking in any way in her eyes. Perhaps it was unreasonable, but it was true, he acknowledged as he put his hand on the doorknob. It shouldn't matter. He'd done what he'd demanded of himself—he had changed his appearance, his business was thriving. He'd even managed a few whirlwind relationships along the way. Yet somehow being with Katie seemed to reduce all of it down to a common denominator—he'd done it to escape the vulnerable boy he'd been, and he hadn't been able to exorcise it completely, not with Katie as a reminder. There was still that tiny bit of insecurity that nothing had really changed at all.

He pasted a nervous smile on his face and opened the door. Katie stood on the grey concrete step, a tray with two large coffees in one hand and her briefcase in the other. She looked tall and graceful in a simple wrap-around skirt and T-shirt. He swallowed, more affected by her appearance than he cared to admit. Trying to stick to business was going to be difficult.

"Good morning."

"Hi. May I come in?"

"Oh, of course!" Belatedly, he stepped back, allowing her to enter. "Did you have any trouble finding the place?"

Katie stepped in and handed Ric the tray of coffee. She hadn't had any trouble with the address, but instead had gaped at the affluent homes in the area as she drove through the winding streets. Every one of them cost more than she could ever afford in a lifetime, complete with well-kept yards. Ric's home was stunning from the outside, huge with lots of grey stonework, dark grey siding, and deep burgundy shutters. Taking a look through the foyer, she saw the inside was as beautiful as the out. Everything in her field of vision was spotlessly clean, and she saw brushed chrome stools lined up beside a granite-topped eating nook. Nothing was ostentatious, but everything she could see had an air of quality about it.

"I didn't have any trouble at all. This is a lovely area."

"I've got a great view, too. Come on in. I could use that coffee." He gestured with the tray in his hand.

She slid off her sandals, wary of tracking dirt into his spotless house. Now her feet were bare except for a simple toe ring and she heard the sound of their soles on the hardwood floor as he led her to the kitchen. The fringed hem of her skirt grazed her ankles as she took a seat on a bar stool at the nook. She watched silently as Ric turned his back to her, taking the cups out of the cardboard tray. His shoulders shifted, contouring the white shirt to their form and pulling it taut against his back, making her mouth suddenly go dry. Dropping her gaze, she realized he was wearing faded jeans again. Really, how could one man be so attractive, and yet not show any signs of vanity?

She spoke to ease the tension running through her veins. "Um. I got you cream and sugar. I hope that's okay."

"That's perfect." Ric flipped back the spouts, handing her a cup. His gaze met hers across the counter, and her throat tightened. She had to be crazy. Because right now she couldn't care less about coffee. What she really wanted to do was undo those buttons on his shirt and get to the skin underneath.

Her body flushed as she looked away. Why, oh why was it that every time he looked at her, it seemed as though he had questions he wasn't asking?

"Cheers," he offered, and she laughed tightly as they touched rims. They'd tinkled glasses a lot as children, drinking sparkling juice at social events while their parents drank spirits. Back then it had been simple childish fun and not fraught with complications like it was now.

"I've got all the paperwork ready," he said after his first sip.

Katie removed the lid from her cup and blew on the surface, watching him over the rim. His shirt was trendy yet understated and showed off the hints of ripples in his shoulders and arms. Briefly she wondered what it would be like to be held in such strong arms, resting her head on his solid chest. And bare feet in jeans…he couldn't realize how sexy that was, surely. Her fingers itched again as she imagined how he'd look in nothing but the jeans. She squirmed from the discomfort of that arousing thought. *Think of something else,* she commanded herself, struggling to remember why she was here.

She took a drink of coffee and replied, "I've also got a list of everything that needs our attention and a basic timeline of what needs to be completed when. I thought today would be a good time since we have a better chance at not being interrupted."

Not being interrupted. Now there was a thought to cause even more discomfort.

Besides, I can't stop staring at your feet, she thought, but kept her mouth shut as she studied his arches. She'd been here before and let it cloud her judgment. All she had to do was exert a little self-control. It was simple, wasn't it?

"Come on into the den then," he suggested, and she followed him out of the kitchen and into the most amazing room she'd ever seen.

On the north side, a window covered most of one wall, letting in lots of light without the glare of direct sun. On the side closest to the foyer was a huge computer workstation and printer table in lovely oak, complemented by a plump leather chair. The other two walls were covered in oak bookshelves. Beneath the shelves on the east wall sat a black leather sofa. A matching oak coffee table graced the middle of the room, sheaves of paper arranged neatly on its top.

"Wow. You must love working in here." She stood in the doorway and simply admired, ruing the fact that her tiny apartment hardly had enough room for her tiny department store desk and basic computer. As it was they were tucked into a corner of her bedroom.

"I don't always like working at the office" he admitted. "This is more homey and comfortable." He gestured to the sofa. "I've got everything laid out here. Have a seat."

Katie sank into the sofa and sighed. Soft, buttery leather caressed her skin as the rich scent of the fabric surrounded her. It was much better than a hard old desk chair. "Oh. My. I might never want to leave," she breathed in contentment.

A strange look came across Ric's face, but he quickly shuttered it away. Oh dear, had she said the wrong thing again? She sat up straighter. It was bad enough she was beginning to indulge in fantasies. She didn't need to give him fuel for the same.

"Let's get started," she said firmly, and he took his place beside her, clicking open his pen and grabbing the first stack of papers.

Much later, Katie checked her watch, astonished to find two hours had passed. The coffee was long gone and papers lay strewn everywhere. They had made it through the first two pages of her checklist, and she rubbed a hand along the back of her neck and sighed.

"Time for a break?"

"I can't believe it's half-past twelve," she groaned, flexing her neck from side to side. "We got caught up in the work and I lost track of time."

At that precise moment, Ric's stomach grumbled in the stillness and Katie snorted out her nose. Ric chuckled as they leaned back against the cushiony softness of the sofa. Their heads turned automatically, like a flower turns to the sun. The look he gave her was warm and uncomplicated.

"I think I should offer you some lunch."

She smiled. "That sounds nice. Besides, we got a lot done this morning. It's amazing what you can accomplish when you have a solid block of time to simply work at it."

Ric held out a hand and helped her to her feet. "We can finish up the last of it later," he suggested. "Why don't you go out on the deck? I'll fix something and bring it out."

They wandered through the kitchen and Ric slid the balcony door open for her.

"Are you sure you don't need any help?" she offered, but he shook his head.

"Nope. You relax. It won't be fancy, though. I'm not much of a chef."

"I don't need fancy," she murmured, her hand still on the door frame, and for a moment, their gazes met. There was the pull again, the one that made her want to abandon all caution and find out what it would be like to be held by those fabulous arms, pressed against him skin to skin.

Quietly, she stepped away and moved to the railing of the deck, out of his reach and away from those eyes that seemed to see way too much for comfort.

The view of the valley was breathtaking. The deck fell away to a backyard of rich green grass, and beyond the fence lay acres of wild grass and flowers. Small wild shrubs dotted the rough landscape, and she could well imagine deer wandering through in the pre-dawn dimness, or jackrabbits bounding out of the way of a marauding coyote. Beyond the wildness, she saw the pale grey-blue stripe of the TransCanada Highway, then the green-grey of the rolling foothills, leading to a spectacular view of the Rockies, long and winding and jaggedly majestic. It was comforting, yet somehow remote, and Katie wondered if Ric knew how much his choice of home reflected who he was. She could spend hours out here, simply looking at all the wide-open space. Sighing, she leaned against the wood railing and tapped her bare toe on the smooth decking. Ric's house wasn't glamorous, but it was certainly large, well cared for and well situated. She could understand why he chose it. And it was a million-dollar reminder of the differences in their positions.

Ric slid the knife through the bread and took a deep breath to calm himself. He saw Katie through the sliding doors. She was leaning over the railing of the deck, looking at the view. As he placed the bread in a basket, he watched as her foot slid back from beneath her skirt and began tapping carelessly against the floor of the deck. She tipped her head back, basking in the noon light, and his hands halted. He watched her for a long moment, entranced by the tiniest movements; her hair falling down her back, the way her weight shifted to her left hip as her right heel moved back and forth.

Damn. He cared about her again. More than simply proving himself to her, more than just the attraction he felt in her presence or the enjoyment of butting heads. No, it was a deep-seated feeling of longing, of caring, of tenderness. Of wanting to simply spend time together, without business or the past between them. They hadn't talked about *things* since they'd reconnected. It was always about the business with her. Perhaps he could change that, learn more about what made Katie, the woman, tick. And perhaps she'd wonder the same thing, and he could explain all of it.

He placed the breadbasket on a tray, checked its contents and was satisfied. Going to the door, he tapped once and she came over to slide it open for him.

"There's a bottle of wine and glasses on the nook," he explained, taking the tray to the glass topped table at the south corner of the deck. "Would you mind grabbing them?"

"Not at all," she replied, and while she was gone, he arranged the food on the table along with linen napkins.

She returned and poured the wine while he shut the patio door behind her.

Coming up behind her, he reached around her intimately as he picked up his glass. "To the Pick and Choose," His voice was no more than a breath. "And its wonderful management team."

Ric touched his glass to hers, disheartened when she turned away from the proximity of their bodies when what he wanted was to feel the warmth hovering between them.

"I'm afraid I can't compete with your culinary skills."

"Don't be silly. It looks wonderful," Katie admonished gently, taking her seat. Once she sat, Ric followed suit and told her to help herself.

What he lacked in ability he made up for in variety. The offerings were simple but delicious. Crusty French bread, thin slices of roast beef, various cheeses, and roasted peppers and zucchini. A smaller plate held raw vegetables and there was a bowl of fresh strawberries and blueberries for dessert.

Katie bit into a pepper, running the tip of her tongue over her lips. "Oh, this is delicious," she said appreciatively.

"I'm glad you approve," Ric replied, filling his own plate from the selection.

The tension dissipated in the mellow warmth of the sun. They ate in companionable silence, with the shush of the breeze and the song of the birds weaving a spell around them. Katie leaned back and cradled her wine glass. It was a particularly fine red and she was sipping and savouring. She watched Ric with hooded eyes. Why on earth did this feel so *right* when she was obviously in the wrong place? She and Ric were from different worlds now. He was the rich exec, and she hadn't been anything but a waitress for the last decade.

"You have a lovely spot," she commented, liking it despite herself.

"My parents thought it odd I didn't choose one of my own developments." He smiled crookedly into his glass like he was keeping a secret. "But I saw this place and loved it. It's quiet and the view…well, it can't be beat. After lunch I can give you the rest of the tour if you like."

"I'd like that a lot. Your kitchen and dining room are as big as my entire apartment." She said it as much to remind herself as him. She did not belong in a mansion. It was some warped trick of fate that she was here in the first place.

Ric picked up a strawberry and turned it over in his fingers before taking a bite. "True," he admitted, "but this place is too big for one person. I only lasted a week before I knew I had to share it with someone."

Katie's heart plummeted and she didn't want to admit the reason why. Ric was living with someone? He'd never mentioned it. But then, why would he? They'd both made it clear their personal lives weren't part of the equation. Avoiding his eyes, she stood.

"Let me help you clean this up," she murmured, and began stacking plates and empty dishes on the tray. She felt Ric's gaze on her but kept her mouth shut. She knew as sure as anything that if she spoke she'd make a complete ass of herself.

He opened the door for her and she took the tray to the counter beside the sink.

Simply to keep her hands busy, she began loading the dirty dishes into the dishwasher, until she felt something soft and furry twining about her ankles. She looked down and saw a black ball of fluff preening up against her legs.

She looked up at Ric and he smiled widely. "Katie, this is Gilligan. My housemate."

She knelt down and rubbed a hand over the cat's back, smiling as he arched his back into her palm. "He's lovely," she said, stroking Gilligan as he purred.

"He sheds and he's a fussy eater," Ric complained, but when Katie looked at him the same smile lit his face. "I can't imagine not having him now."

Katie stood. Wow, a cat. It made Ric seem even more human. Not many single guys she knew could be bothered with caring for a pet. And yet...she got the feeling that having Gilligan around made the house less empty. She had no right to feel relieved that it was a cat he shared his life with, but she was just the same.

She pictured Ric sitting alone in the evening with only Gilligan for company and felt an odd constriction around her heart.

"How about that tour?" she asked.

As Ric showed her the rest of the house, two things became abundantly clear. First of all, this house was built for a family. And secondly, Ric was lonely.

The top floor had four bedrooms and a lounge, the latter equipped with a big screen TV and home theatre system. Three of the bedrooms were large and only one was furnished with a bed—a lonely queen-sized covered with a neutral spread. As her feet sank into the rich carpet, she got the feeling these rooms were waiting...for something, or someone. As she followed him through the upstairs, she peeked into a large, coldly clean bathroom that almost looked like it had never been used. The hall ended with the door to the master bedroom.

She stepped inside his bedroom. The personal nature of the room made it uncomfortable enough, but as she looked around, she felt as though she were witnessing something very private, and very intense.

Ric had decorated his bedroom. Really decorated it, not just filled it with the necessary furniture.

The centrepiece was the bed, and Katie swallowed hard as she stared at it. It was nothing short of decadent, and an image flashed before her, of Ric, and herself, entwined in the covers. The bed was king-sized, a four-poster in dark walnut. His duvet was gold and red silk, the head covered with a selection of gold and red throw pillows in varying rich fabrics. She imagined being held in Ric's arms beneath the silk, and her pulse jumped.

Whoa. She had to leave that explosive picture behind in a hurry. Her cheeks flaming, she turned away. It didn't help. The walls were painted a rich, throbbing red, with vertical stripes of glossy finish paint giving the impression of tapestry. It was opulent and it was sexual and she wasn't immune to its power.

Katie ran a hand over the silky finish of the footboard. "Ric, this room is…" What could she say now? As a teenager, he'd had plain white walls and a navy spread, and his wall had plaques from science fairs and a periodic table pinned up with thumbtacks. They'd laughingly dubbed it the "Passion Pit". All these years later, this room could hold that title and then some. "It's a lot different from your room in high school."

It was a room made for loving. She wondered if he realized how potent it was.

"I didn't decorate the other rooms," he admitted, his voice close to her ear and warm like melted butter. "But the ones I spend the most time in…here, the kitchen, the den…I wanted them done right."

He moved to the end of the room and slid open a door, revealing a huge ensuite and beyond that, a walk in closet as big as her own bedroom.

The phone rang, echoing through the house. "Excuse me for a moment," he said, and disappeared on silent feet.

She stepped inside the ensuite onto ceramic tile. On her right was a double shower, a toilet, a makeup counter and mirror that had to be at least five feet long. It turned a corner to become a double sink and mirror with an oak vanity beneath. But the glory of the room was the Jacuzzi, a two-person jetted tub surrounded by gold veined marble and with gold fixtures.

These rooms—his private rooms—were made for two. The huge, opulent bed, the shower for two. The make-up mirror and length of drawers. It was made for a couple, rising in the morning and getting ready side by side. It was made for steamy showers late at night, and long, seductive bubbles with candles and champagne. His bedroom and the ensuite screamed seduction, and Katie realized that deep down Ric had a tender, romantic heart despite his sometimes cold appearance. She wondered what would happen if he released all the passion he seemed to hold behind his stiff exterior. She wondered what it would be like if she were on the receiving end, and her muscles tightened in anticipation.

If he tried to seduce her right now, she knew she'd abandon all willpower and good sense and go for it.

Katie backed out of the room, feeling both longing and an accompanying fear. He was waiting for her in the hall, his face naked of all pretense. Suddenly she knew beyond a doubt he'd wanted her to see this, to see how he lived. His eyes held emotions she didn't want to acknowledge. It was longing and wanting and waiting for her to make a move. Oh God, he couldn't know how badly she wanted to make that move.

As their gazes caught and held, she somehow knew what she had no right to ask. The empty rooms, the extra space not needed for one person....deep inside she knew he'd bought this house wishing for a family of his own. And that was something they differed on. She had things to prove before she even thought about a husband and kids. The very thought terrified her. Ric had already proven himself. He'd become the success he'd vowed he would, but she hadn't even begun.

Looking at him now, she could well imagine him rocking a baby daughter or pitching a ball to a toddler holding a bat twice his size. It was a beautiful picture.

The world seemed made for those going two by two and for a fleeting moment, Katie understood why. A husband, children, all the every day things many took for granted but remained elusive for others. She'd never wanted that for herself, until now, picturing Ric as a father. He'd be the hands-on type too, the kind who would tuck them into bed and then spend an hour relaxing with his wife in deepening twilight, winding down with some one on one time. It was a pure silly fantasy that had her picturing herself as his wife. And she couldn't afford to think that way. She had a restaurant to get off the ground...and running it wasn't going to leave her any spare time for a long time to come.

They were still gazing into each other's eyes and Katie felt her pulse leap and take off running. She had to come up with something to say, and lamely tried, "Your house is gorgeous." It was stating the obvious and she inwardly winced. She made the mistake of looking down at Ric's feet again, the bare toes surrounded by rich carpet. She'd never seen toes so seductive in all her life.

His right foot lifted and took a step forward...the left came to meet it, and he stood a whisper away, so close they were almost touching as his chest rose and fell with his breathing.

"I'm glad you like it," he murmured.

She couldn't look up. She couldn't. Oh God, why did he have to be so good-looking and successful and kind and funny and sexy?

His hand lifted and the warmth of his fingers caressed her hair. He rubbed the strands between his fingers as her heart thundered, remembering. "You always had the most beautiful hair," he murmured, and her eyes slammed closed.

Touch me, she thought, her body leaning in towards his.

His fingers slid up her arm and under the waterfall of hair at her neck. His breath heated her cheek as his lips barely brushed the surface, while her chest rose and fell torturously. His lips slid closer to her mouth, soft, tantalizing.

"I can't do this," she choked, and took a step back suddenly, leaving his hand in the air where her head had been. What was she thinking? She couldn't let things get physical with Ric. When things got physical, they also got emotional. All the lines got blurred and she got hurt. Her heart pounded almost painfully; Ric hadn't moved since she'd blurted out that she couldn't go through with it. Katie made the mistake of looking up at him and felt the terrible urge to forget about all her misgivings and launch herself into his arms. To kiss him then and there and see exactly where it might lead.

But that would be wrong, for both of them.

Chapter Six

She steeled herself. "I can't, Ric. Oh, damn."

He lowered his hand and put it in his pocket, his jaw hard as iron, eyes cold. "I see."

"No, I don't think you do. Oh please, can we go back downstairs? I can't think straight." She wiped her hand down her cheek. Distance. She needed to put physical distance between them.

"If that's what you want."

His tone was cool and the bite of guilt gnawed into her as she followed him back down the carpeted stairs. She felt safer in the neutral atmosphere of the kitchen where things were functional and not intimate.

Ric leaned against the nook and folded his arms, and she knew by his remoteness, the way his jaw was clamped shut and his eyes closed off, she'd hurt his feelings. That was the last thing she wanted to do. She'd hurt him once before and didn't want to repeat it. She had to explain, to make him see. Make him see it wasn't a case of her rejecting him, but of her protecting herself plain and simple.

"Please don't be mad," she pleaded.

"I don't understand," he said slowly, as if deliberately trying to keep his voice level. "I could swear I've been getting signals from you."

Signals? Oh, if he only knew. One minute she was choking on her own breath, exchanging longing gazes, and the next she was putting distance between them or picking a fight. She'd been feeling like a silly teenager ever since they'd met again, feeling constantly like a stop and go light where he was concerned.

She sighed. She'd fallen for someone she worked with once before with disastrous consequences, professionally and personally.

"Then I'm afraid you misread."

Ric's arms uncrossed and she saw a muscle clench in his jaw. He *was* mad, and had every reason. Her eyes widened as his darkened in anger, narrowed and dangerous.

"Misread? You're telling me I imagined what happened upstairs just now?"

It was like old times. Katie had been very good at it in the past. Be sweet enough, intimate enough to keep him interested, then push him away when he got too close. Frustration bubbled away, both sexual and emotional. He was getting sick and tired of being Katie Buick's puppet. He'd been insecure in every relationship he'd had since, wondering if he was really what his partner wanted or if they only saw the package he'd put together. Katie had done that to him. He'd lacked the courage to confront her about it ten years ago, but he wasn't that boy any longer. He took a step closer to her and she shriveled back into herself.

"I was there, Katie!" He grabbed her upper arms, drawing her closer. "I felt your heart pounding, the way you leaned into my body! Misread? Ha!"

"All right! You're right!" she exploded, stumbling backward, away from his grip and hard, unyielding body.

"You're admitting it. It's about time." He took a step forward, his gaze fixed on her lips. This time he wouldn't be timid. He'd kiss her and be done with it.

"Don't," she warned him, holding up her hands.

He took another step but backed off when he looked into her eyes. They weren't angry...they were frightened. And that was where he drew the line. "Then tell me why."

She swore it would never happen again. It wasn't something she was proud of and only a handful of people even knew what had happened, but faced with Ric's current anger and their past, she knew he deserved to understand where she was coming from.

"I made the mistake of getting involved with a co-worker once," she admitted on a huge breath. Admitting it brought the humiliation back, fresh and painful, and she blinked back hot tears. She would not cry over this again. Resolute, she swallowed the hard lump in her throat and lifted her chin. "I now have a personal policy not to ever mix business with pleasure."

"And I'm business."

"Strictly. We've already signed the papers saying so. I can't...no, I won't, be involved with my business partner."

His shoulders relaxed, his face less harsh. She couldn't help being relieved the worst of the storm seemed over and that his anger had diffused quickly. He seemed to understand a little and it meant a great deal to her.

"It's not personal, Ric. I just...this business is everything to me and I can't let anything get in the way of that."

"What happened?"

"Sorry?"

"I mean, what did he do that made you determined not to go there again?" Ric pulled out a bar stool and sat, resting his arms on the breakfast nook.

Was she actually in Ric Emerson's kitchen, and was he prompting her to talk about past romantic failures? This had to be some parallel universe, because not in a million years could she have pictured it. He wasn't judging her or pumping her for juicy details. He was being a friend and it was the one sure way of sneaking beneath her self-constructed armour.

She went to the nook, ignored the other stool and rested her elbows on the brown marble top instead.

"I was working for a chain at the time. We had a new owner coming in and the manager's job was up for grabs. We were both assistant managers at the time. I got caught up in him, he got caught up in the new opportunity, romanced the new boss and convinced her I'd dipped into the till a few times. I was out of a job, out of a recommendation, and nursing a broken heart. That's the long and short of it."

There was more, much more, but there was only so much she could reveal and still keep her dignity. She'd given him enough that he could understand...and perhaps keep any sort of good opinion he'd formed about her.

"That's the whole story?"

He was looking at her like he expected more, and she wondered if he'd picked up on how guilty she felt inside. He couldn't possibly know the rest of it; and she wasn't going to tell him. If he knew, he'd regret ever going into business with her. Worse, she'd be faced with his disappointment. For years, his opinion hadn't mattered, but now it did. She'd keep the rest of the truth and simply try to build on what they already had.

"Yeah, that's it."

To her relief, he handed her a glass, the ice tinkling softly. "You don't think I'd do something like that, do you?"

"No, I don't. You've always had too much integrity for that. You're the most honest person I know." She couldn't help but hate that perfection as much as she admired it.

"But you blame yourself because you think you should have seen. You don't trust yourself."

She was surprised he understood and her posture stiffened in defense. "Emotional attachments cloud my judgment. That's why I don't mix them with work. And that works for me."

Working with Ric was refreshing yet a bit bitter at the same time. He knew how to be a friend, understood more than she cared to admit, yet the past always seemed to taint things. Her stomach churned; her emotions had been on a rollercoaster far too long. "I'm afraid I'm not feeling too much like work anymore. I think I'll get my stuff together and head home, if you don't mind."

"Not at all. We got a lot done this morning. Besides, there's always e-mail and telephones, and it's not like my office is far from the shop if you need anything."

Katie retrieved her bag from the office and when she came out Ric was waiting at the door. "Katie?"

She looked up and found him staring down at her so earnestly she almost forgot what she was about. It was as if he *knew*, like he could see right inside of her, and it made her want to spill out the whole sordid story of what Craig had actually done to her. She clamped her mouth shut. If he knew, any friendship they'd forged would go right out the window. She waited for what he was going to say.

"Thanks for telling me."

He lifted his hand and touched her face, his thumb rubbing her jaw gently. She attempted a smile but failed. He was nearly perfect...she would never measure up to his ideal. It would be better for both of them if they kept meetings in neutral territory after this.

"Thanks for lunch. I'll be in touch."

She left him in the open doorway, and try as she might, the picture of him there in his lonely house followed her all the way home.

℥ ℣

Katie rose, placing her hands on the small of her back and stretching out the permanent kink sitting there. A local radio station pumped out the latest hip-hop from a small stereo on the counter. She sighed, running a hand over her ponytail and seeing a fluff of white dust erupt around her head.

She'd thought she was finished with crack filling, until the idiots delivering furniture yesterday left a huge gouge in the wall. She'd plastered it this morning, and tonight went to work sanding it and prepping the wall to repaint. Unfortunately, by spending the evening alone with only the radio keeping her company, her thoughts kept drifting to Ric.

That day at his house affected her more than she wanted to admit. Looking into his eyes, she'd never wanted anything as much as she wanted to kiss him, to let her fingers run through those short curls and feel his body close to hers. She hadn't counted on a physical attraction this potent. She had never felt anything like that for him in years past. And it wasn't his money, or his power, or his smoldering looks. It was more elemental than that. It was a basic, person-to-person recognition.

It wasn't going to happen. She shook her head, scrubbing the drywall with renewed vigor. As much as she was confident in her ability to run the restaurant, she was equally certain that she was a disaster at personal relationships. She'd never forgive herself if she screwed up the Pick and Choose because she couldn't be objective. She'd have to be satisfied with fantasies of him. As long as she didn't act on the attraction, she was safe.

A knock sounded at the door and she jumped guiltily, shaken abruptly from the romantic interlude playing in her head. Peering out the window, she saw Ric's figure and felt her body flush. In her fantasy, they'd been pressed close together, his lips firm on hers as he peeled away...

Now he was here in the flesh. Forcing deep breaths, she hurried to unlock the door as he knocked a second time.

Ric stepped over the threshold, bigger than life and looking devastatingly delicious in a navy suit and light blue shirt. His tie was knotted up tightly so the collar of his shirt lay snug and flat. He looked like an ad from a magazine and Katie felt a bubble of anticipation in her belly. Her recent fantasy involved peeling him out of a similar suit, layer by tailored layer, and she knew she dare not say anything or she'd embarrass herself completely. She needed to put space between them.

"You look like a ghost." He reached out and touched the tip of her nose with a finger, and she was reminded of how he'd caressed her face as she'd left his house. She shied away. When he drew back his hand, the fingertip was dotted with drywall dust.

"I'm repairing. I still have to paint."

Ric took a paper bag from behind his back and placed it on the now yellow-tinged counter. "Want some help?"

She looked down his suit and shrugged, trying desperately to look dismissive. "I doubt you're going to paint in your designer suit."

His brows pulled together at the snap of irritation in her voice. "It's only a suit."

That was one of the big differences between them. To him, it was just clothing. To her, it represented several hundred dollars she wouldn't dare tarnish since she couldn't afford to replace it. Her lips thinned. "Whatever. They're your clothes."

The song changed to something with a rock beat and Ric angled an eyebrow at her. "Maybe you'd like something to eat first."

His tone clearly suggested perhaps her attitude was caused by hunger, and she tried to relax. Besides, now that he mentioned it, something definitely smelled beefy and greasy in the paper sack. How long had it been since she'd eaten a fast-food burger? She'd concentrated a long time on abolishing junk food from her diet, and here was Ric, tempting her with all the things she knew were bad for her.

Give it up, Katie, she chided herself. A burger was only a burger after all.

"How did you know I was here?"

He reached in the bag and took out two foil-wrapped burgers and two paper sacks of fries. "I called your apartment. When you didn't answer, I figured here would be the best bet. There's only three days left until opening. I know you assured me you had things under control, but with time being short…"

"Don't remind me." Katie went to the other end of the room and grabbed two chairs while Ric picked up a small table and put it in the middle of the room.

"Do you have ketchup?"

She raised one eyebrow. "No fries on our menu, or burgers either. No ketchup."

"We'll have to do without, I guess," he lamented, sitting on the dusty chair without a flicker of concern about his trousers or his arteries.

Katie unwrapped her sandwich and stared at it. How many grams of fat were in it? Forty? Fifty? Too many. Add in the cheese, and was that a strip of bacon peeking out from beneath the bun? And mayo too, she thought with dismay.

"Something wrong with your burger?"

She smiled faintly. "No." She would not deliver a speech at this moment about the evils of fast food. Besides, she hadn't eaten since this morning and it smelled too good to resist. She took a bite. It was juicy and her taste buds rejoiced, popping at the vinegary pucker of sour pickles. Why was it everything she didn't want or need had to be so good?

"Seems a bit ironic, doesn't it?" she commented, putting down her burger and examining a long, golden french fry. "I'm opening a healthy choices restaurant and sit here eating burgers and fries, my very competition."

"Sometimes you need a good burger," Ric decreed. "Everything in moderation, right?"

"Not if we want to make a profit," she replied dryly, but despite herself took another scrumptious bite.

He wiped his hands on a paper napkin and looked around. "Despite that wall, the place looks good, Katie."

"My to-do list is still a mile long. I don't feel like I'm ever going to be ready."

"We'll be ready."

She looked up, startled by the tone of absolute confidence in his voice. At the warmth of his gaze, she looked down. "I don't know…" she trailed off.

"I do. You've worked hard, covered your bases. I know opening day will be a hit."

She concentrated on her fries, drawing circles on her wrapper with a golden tip. She was deeply touched at his faith in her and unsure how to accept it gracefully. "I have to clean this place up, arrange the furniture, make sure my deliveries are on schedule, hook up the cash register, make sure the debit card and credit links work…there's so much potential for things to go wrong."

Ric balled up his napkin and tossed it into the paper bag. "Success happens when opportunity meets preparation. You've got the opportunity, and I've never seen anyone more bent on being prepared. You'll do fine."

She had a difficult time accepting his praise. She stood, avoiding his gaze. "I'm thirsty. I've got some iced tea in the cooler. Want one?"

"Sure."

She took ten deep breaths as she went behind the counter to get the drinks. For the few weeks following their near-kiss, she'd been able to keep a business-like distance between them, but now, tonight, he showed up at the empty restaurant bearing dinner. She'd tried hard not to truly be alone with him. Lord, she had enough to worry about without getting all nerved up over Ric.

She handed him his beverage, turning the bottle to make sure their fingers didn't touch. "Why did you come by, really?"

"To see if you needed help. This is a partnership, you know, and with opening day being so soon—I thought I might be of some use." He grinned at her, a crooked little slice that grabbed at her heart. "I would have come sooner, but I've been up to my eyebrows in a new development, and I was out of town for a few days."

"You're of no use to me in that get-up." She swigged her tea straight from the bottle and nodded at his jacket, challenging.

"Say the word and it's gone."

Iced tea started down her windpipe as she choked, and the resulting spate of coughing had Ric laughing with glee. "Loosen up, Katie. You're a bundle of nerves. Relax. Things will go fine."

If only he knew. She tried to scowl at him as she re-capped the bottle. It wasn't opening day making her nervous right now. It was him, and his GQ appearance, his chocolate eyes with the delicious crinkles at the corners. He was still smiling as he wiggled off his tie and put his suit jacket over the back of the chair. Her throat closed over. Could he possibly know how much she wanted him? She hoped not. Things were difficult enough.

"What can I do?" He rolled his sleeves back, revealing tanned, muscular arms.

"There's a vacuum in the back. You can clean up the dust while I get the paint."

"Consider it done."

For an hour, they worked together, talking little, and the physical labour dispelled some of the tension throbbing through Katie's body. Ric sometimes sang softly along with the radio. Once, Katie looked over her shoulder as she filled the roller with terracotta paint and saw his butt give a little wiggle with the music as he leaned over to unplug the vacuum. She snorted, but turned back, concentrating on the wall when Ric spun to see what was funny.

"What are you laughing at?"

She concentrated on smoothing the roller over the wall, struggling to keep a straight face. "Oh, nothing."

"Like hell." He wound the cord up to the vacuum and sauntered over. "Tell me."

"Nope. I don't even remember," she replied, her face deadpan.

A sash brush, covered in red paint, appeared two inches from her cheek.

"You have a problem with my dancing?"

Roll, roll, went the paint on the wall.

The brush tipped her cheek, leaving a splotch of paint.

She spun, her eyes full of fun as she lifted the roller menacingly. "Bad move, preppy boy."

He laughed, brandishing the brush to keep her back. "You wouldn't dare."

She stalked him, pinning him with the feral gleam in her eyes. "How much did that shirt cost you, Ric? Pocket change, right?"

"Look, don't do anything cr…"

He didn't get a chance to finish. She caught up with him and, cool as a cucumber, rolled the paint from his chest to his navel while his mouth dropped open.

She backed off, covering her mouth with a hand, shocked at her behaviour and laughing at the amazed expression on his face.

His eyebrows gathered menacingly as his lips curved up in a cunning smile. Without saying a word, he undid the top button of his shirt. The second, and the third.

Panic bubbled inside her. She'd imagined him shirtless in her fantasies but she wasn't ready for the reality. She got the distinct feeling she was playing with fire and about to get burned, big time. She caught a glimpse of dark chest hair as his fingers reached the fourth button, and she stammered, "Wh- what are you doing?"

"You've ruined my shirt," he stated matter-of-factly. "I'm taking it off."

"You can't do that," she blurted out, spinning away to put her roller back in the tray. She heard his mocking laughter behind her and cursed silently, hating the fact he knew exactly what buttons to push to knock her off-balance. Thankfully, when she turned back, he had his shirt buttoned again, the paint already drying to a darker brick colour against the light background.

Thankfully, Ric didn't push the issue and the joke was over. She began wiping down the counters, filled a bucket with soapy water, and they started cleaning and arranging tables. Ric found a stud in the wall and hung the daily specials board, a wood-framed chalkboard. Katie put a box of chalk on the counter beside it, took out one long piece and wrote:

OPENING SPECIALS

That was all. She already knew what the specials would be, but she'd write them on Monday morning, when she opened for the very first time. Putting the chalk down, she brushed off her hands and stood back.

"It's starting to look like a restaurant around here." Ric shoved his hands in his pockets and surveyed the room. "You were right about the colours. It's warm and inviting. I like the furniture too. Heavy as the dickens, though." The table and chairs were constructed of iron, like patio chairs in a small café. She'd tried very hard to make it casually intimate, despite the cafeteria-style method of service. She'd added a wider sill to the large front window, and potted trees and plants were waiting to sit there, beneath the neon "Open" sign.

"I like it too."

"Well." Ric looked around, then checked his watch. "It's nearly ten. That's a good evening's work."

Ten, already? With Ric standing near, her body felt energized, her mind alert. Her senses were sharper somehow and she was anything but sleepy, even though she knew she needed rest if she weren't going to be a zombie on opening day.

"The time went fast," she offered lamely.

A slow song came on the radio, and when Ric smiled at her, Katie's resolve faltered. *Don't ask me to dance,* she prayed.

"Wanna dance?"

Oh, shoot.

He held out a hand and she didn't know what to do. Her hesitation must have been obvious because Ric looked at her meaningfully and cajoled, "It's just a dance, Katie. We've done it before."

Of course. At the country club. They were teenagers and two out of a handful of young people there. Occasionally, they'd be pressed into dancing. It hadn't been unpleasant. But Ric hadn't raised her temperature then, not as he did now.

She took his hand and her body shivered as he took her into his arms. His hand pressed against her waist, drawing her closer as they circled the floor with tiny steps. Beat by beat, all her resolve melted until she leaned into him, her head resting lightly on his right shoulder. He brought their hands in so they rested on his chest, and she felt the erratic beating of his heart against her fingers. His body was warm and hard and for the first time in years, Katie felt a security there, like she was cherished and protected.

It was easy to rest here, to let herself forget how hard it was to prove herself. She forgot all the disparaging words and skeptical looks when she said she was starting her own business. She could escape that loathsome title—Girl Most Likely to Have Fun—and simply be Katie, the woman. She hadn't ever been that person before, and it filled her with sweetness.

The song ended, but she was still in his arms, her eyes closed, feeling his chest rise and fall with his breathing as their feet still shuffled along. The DJ droned on and commercials blared through the speakers, but it didn't register. Ric dropped his head and she felt his lips against her hair as he kissed the top of her dusty head.

"Katie," he whispered. Without warning, he dipped his head further and captured her lips with his.

They were warm and persuasive, tinted with the taste of iced tea. His tongue slipped inside and she met it, letting him take the lead and following willingly. Their feet stopped moving and they stood still while her arms slid up over his shoulder blades.

It was all she'd imagined, and more. He was firm but gentle, solid and sure, and his quiet command of her mouth made her feel more feminine than she had in a long time. Kissing Ric just fit.

His hand moved from her shoulder down, down to capture her breast in his palm.

It was like a bucket of cold water doused her. She pulled away from him, out of the spell and away from the warmth of his arms. She hugged her elbows close to her sides.

His expression was unreadable. "Sorry. Didn't mean to break the rules."

"Didn't you?"

He laughed tightly. "Maybe. But you weren't exactly fighting me off. You wanted to as much as I did."

But it was exactly what she wanted and not what she needed. He couldn't possibly know that, nor could she tell him and give him the power of that knowledge. Blessedly, Katie's cell phone rang, preventing her from having to come up with a response when she was completely rattled. "Excuse me a moment."

She answered, spoke for a minute, then putting her hand over the mouthpiece, said, "It's the transport company. We've got problems with a shipment I have to sort out." She turned back to the phone and disappeared into the back of the building and the office housed there, leaving him standing in the middle of the dusty floor alone.

When she came back ten minutes later, he had tidied up the tables and chairs and put the vacuum behind the counter. His hands were covered with red paint as he washed up the paint tray in the huge stainless steel sink.

"You're still here," she said, surprised.

"There was still work to do, and it's late." He concentrated on cleaning the roller, squeezing out all the water and paint.

"I didn't expect…" she faltered.

He smiled to himself. That was her problem. She didn't expect. She didn't have any expectations. She was used to people walking away. He knew firsthand how that felt. But he wasn't walking away from her either professionally or personally.

"Just giving you a demonstration," he replied, drying his hands on a paper towel and tossing it in the garbage can.

"Of what?"

Putting the tray away neatly, he went back out in front of the counter and grabbed his suit coat. "Mixing business and pleasure," he replied, tossing her a quick smile. He left, but couldn't resist calling out behind him, "See you in three days."

Chapter Seven

What had he been thinking? Ric gripped the steering wheel and shook his head, calling himself a fool. Showing up at the restaurant had been one thing. They'd worked together just fine. The little paint interlude had been fun too, like a bit of teenage foreplay. He'd enjoyed making her squirm a little, and he smiled in remembrance. Then that song had come on the radio, and she'd looked beautiful, all covered in paint and dust. He hadn't had any choice but to ask her to dance.

What an idiot. Katie had made it perfectly clear she wasn't willing for there to be anything more between them, and the first time he got the chance, he had her in his arms.

And damn, it had felt good. Worse than that, it had felt right. He'd kissed the daylights out of her, touched her, and she'd frozen. When her cell phone rang, he took the opportunity to try to show her he could still be her partner while wanting something more.

He slapped a hand on the wheel, speeding up as he climbed the hill towards his house in the near-darkness. They were business partners. And they worked together well, he could tell already that things were running without a hitch. Why would he jeopardize that, risk having her turn him away for good?

He pressed a button and the garage door slid slowly open. The answer was simple.

He rested his head on the wheel briefly as the door slid down and quieted. He was as attracted to Katie now as he had been ten years ago, and he still somehow hoped he stood some kind of a chance to be with her. Perhaps many would ask why, if they only looked at the surface. But he knew the real Katie, the compassionate girl who had made an awkward boy feel important. The woman who had insecurities about herself and was working hard to overcome them.

Perhaps he should cut his losses and move on, work on making the Pick and Choose successful and forget about anything deeper with Katie. Why would she want him anyway? He hadn't totally shaken off the feelings of Ric Emerson, class geek. He still felt awkward most of the time, still thought mostly of business, and no matter how hard he tried, he still saw flaws when he looked in the mirror. He shut the door to the car and shouldered his briefcase. Stupid, stupid fool.

Now he was bound to her for who knew how long…all the time wanting what he could never have. She'd been clear. Convincing her otherwise was a huge task…even if she did seem to be fighting her feelings every time they turned around. He knew for a fact that you couldn't demand feelings from someone who didn't have them to give.

As Gilligan meowed and twined around his legs, Ric had the thought that he really should get out more and perhaps try dating again. He hadn't done much of that in recent years, keeping himself to friendly dates to fundraisers and various functions. In University, he'd been initiated into a social and sexual life, but it hadn't been satisfying. And he'd never had a long-term relationship. He always had a fear that a woman would see behind his new looks and success and see the unsure teenager beneath. Hardly attractive. He'd been the one who couldn't give his heart to another woman. He hadn't found a woman worthy of it, or perhaps he simply didn't think he was worthy of giving it.

He supposed the only way to conquer his insecurity was to face it, and perhaps dating could be fun. How was he ever going to find the right person if he didn't even look?

He poured food into Gilligan's bowl and rolled down the top of the bag. Problem was, he didn't have to look. He had only ever been truly interested in one woman, a blue-eyed sprite with silken hair. Why couldn't he have her? Just because he used to be a math geek with few social skills and skinny legs didn't mean he didn't have a lot to offer. She'd seen beyond that image once. And perhaps he could convince her to abandon her embargo on business relationships.

What he needed was a plan. A step-by-step plan to show her how much he cared, to make her realize he was the kind of man she needed and could trust.

That was it. He'd make her see he was the kind of man who would love and cherish her and respect her for who she was, without that ridiculous label. He needed to show her she could be a success on her own and their relationship could be separate, taking nothing away from her accomplishments. He needed her to see him for who he was, the way he saw her. He'd forgiven her for turning him down before, even if he hadn't forgotten. Now he had to show her he wanted the woman she'd become.

Motivated, he grabbed a tablet and pen. A plan, yes, that was it. When you embarked on a new venture, you first needed a solid plan, with contingencies built in. That, he knew how to do.

A smile split his face as he felt on familiar ground once more. He'd put it to paper, and then into action.

ဢ ၓ

Katie collapsed on the sofa, exhausted yet still completely wound up. She tucked her hair into a messy ponytail. Opening day had been a hit, a few glitches here and there, a few things that needed smoothing out, but overall, a success.

She pulled her knees into her chest, her light cotton pajama bottoms brushing her cheek as she lowered her head with a sigh. Thank God she'd hired Jenna and Karen. Both had worked with her before and she knew exactly what would entice them away from their current jobs. A work day that ended no later than nine, decent pay, a smoke-free and friendly environment...and they'd worked out splendidly so far. Jenna knew how to cook up a storm while Karen manned the register, took orders, and cleared tables. Katie had kept everything running smoothly, taking notes and doing a bit of everything during the day.

Now, at nine-thirty, she was exhausted and happy. Her feet ached but her heart was full of hope. The trembling trepidation she'd experienced turning on the open sign and unlocking the door was gone. She'd been terrified no one would show up. Instead, at lunchtime she was swamped—every chair had been filled for over an hour and take out orders had been steady.

Her stomach rumbled and she realized that, despite owning a restaurant, she'd forgotten to eat dinner. Around two, she'd grabbed the last square of lasagna from the pan, and a bottle of water. What she needed now was a long bath and something to eat. She had to be up at five-thirty and at the Pick and Choose before seven.

There was a knock at the door and she sighed. What in the world was someone doing here now? Looking out the Judas hole, she saw Ric standing there in his ever-present dark suit. She slid the chain back from the door and opened it.

"Hi," she said, holding the edge of the door with her right hand.

"Hi yourself. Sorry I missed today. We had an accident on the site and I had to be there. Brought you a present though." He was all charm and goodwill as he smiled down at her and her annoyance melted away. Briefly, she resented the fact that he could do that to her with only a smile.

"Come in," she offered, but it came out with little warmth.

"You look exhausted. How did it go?" He stepped into the dining area and put a bottle of champagne on the table as well as a plastic bag.

"We were busy. Really busy," she added, and couldn't help but give a little laugh of wonder. "I'm beat, but we did okay. The place was packed at lunch."

"Congratulations. I knew you could do it."

"Not without your backing." She folded her hands in front of her. He *would* show up while she looked a fright. Oh well. She was too tired to be overly concerned about her appearance.

Ric stepped forward, close enough she smelled his expensive cologne. Close enough she could reach out and touch him.

"All you needed was money and a little direction. All the hard work, the vision, was you, Katie." He tucked a piece of hair behind her ear and her pulse leaped as his fingers grazed her neck.

"I knew I could do it, but I'd hear all the voices of people telling me I was crazy, and I'd start doubting."

"Of course you did. You're human." He dropped his hand and put it in his pocket. "But you carried on, followed through."

His gaze delved deeply into hers as he offered her the one thing she desperately needed.

"I'm proud of you, Katie."

Tears stung her eyes and she looked down. Not once had someone given her those words, such unqualified validation. Her throat swelled and she didn't trust herself to speak.

"Was that patronizing? I didn't mean it to be. I am proud of you. It takes a lot to rise above your insecurities and build something from the beginning."

She cleared her throat. "Like you did?"

He smiled then, and the warmth of it snuggled around her.

"I'm glad you noticed. But yes. I admire your determination. I know it's not easy. But I didn't mean to make you cry."

He tilted up her chin with a finger.

"It's okay," she replied, taking a deep breath and shaking off his hand, showing him she was fine. "I got a little emotional. I'm tired and it's been a long day. You run on adrenaline so long and then when it's gone, you sort of lose it."

"I should have realized." He stepped away, gesturing lamely at the table. "I brought champagne and fruit, thinking we could celebrate, but you're clearly not in the mood for it."

The thought of kicking back with some high-quality bubbly and Ric had a certain appeal. But Katie was sure that after a glass or two, she'd do something stupid like let down her guard and, at the very least, kiss him again, or let him touch her the way he'd started to the other night.

"Thanks for understanding. Right now all I want is a bath and bed."

Liar, her inner voice taunted. Her cheeks coloured as her innocent words took on an intimate meaning. His eyes pinned her for a long moment and she tucked her fingers into her palms to keep from reaching out to him.

"Why don't you sit down, and let me take care of everything," he suggested. He took her arms and pushed her down on to the sofa again. "Relax and give me ten minutes."

Her eyes narrowed suspiciously. "What are you up to?"

"I left you to shoulder the burden of opening day. Now I'm being a good business partner and trying to make up for it."

He disappeared into the bathroom and seconds later, she heard water running and a cupboard door opening and closing. The sound of the water filling the tub had a rhythmic quality and her eyes grew heavy, listening.

Ric came back to the living room and looked around for a moment.

"Nice flowers," he commented, looking at a bouquet of red roses on the table.

"From Dad and Mom. They sent them today as a congratulations."

"May I?" His fingers hovered over a few scarlet blossoms and Katie nodded, wary. What was he going to do with roses?

Sleepy, she burrowed into the cushions and dozed, dimly aware of Ric rummaging through her kitchen. It seemed like only seconds later when he gently shook her shoulder.

"Katie," he murmured, and she opened her eyes.

He was leaning over her and desire pierced her; she fought the urge to grab the end of his tie and pull him down on top of her where he belonged.

Instead he straightened and held out a hand. "Your bath awaits."

Her heart started pounding as she took his hand and let him lead her down the hall. What had he done in her tiny bathroom? And was he seducing her? It was hard to tell with Ric...he was all long looks and light touches. With all the desire snapping between them like sparks, she wasn't sure what he wanted or expected tonight. She wasn't sure what she wanted or expected, either.

Katie turned the corner into the bathroom and caught her breath.

Three thick candles sat on the dark green vanity, their flickering light reflected in the mirror. The calming scent of her lavender bath salts wafted on the moist air and she saw rose petals floating on the water. Her white clothes hamper was pulled close to the edge of the tub, an empty glass and small plate of strawberries and grapes arranged on its top. While her mouth hung open, Ric stepped ahead, undid the wrapper at the top of the bottle and deftly popped the cork. He filled the single glass half full and put the bottle on the floor beside the hamper.

Turning, he met her wide-eyed gaze and she wondered frantically what came next—what she wanted to happen or what she knew should happen.

He took one step, then another, and a third that took him to her side. "Get some rest," he whispered, reaching out to squeeze her forearm, dropping the merest hint of a kiss on her cheek.

He left her there in the bathroom, alone with the warm scents and dusky stillness. Still shocked, she heard the front door shut behind him and she let out a gigantic breath.

He'd done all this for her, expecting nothing in return. Wasn't that a novel thing, now? A half smile curved her lips. Rose petals and champagne and candles. She peeled off her camisole top and slid out of her pajama pants. Dipping one toe in the water, she watched the circles move away from her foot, making the petals rise and fall on the tiny waves. She got all the way in and reached for the champagne, sampled a strawberry.

And wished she were a stronger woman. Because God help her, she was wishing Ric had never walked out that door tonight, and that wasn't good.

෨ ෬

Ric's absence on opening day turned out to be an anomaly. Katie knew and understood he had a large business to run, and didn't expect him to show up every day. Yet after the first day, he called her at least once daily, asking how things were going, if she needed any assistance with anything. In addition to Mark's lawyering skills, Ric also offered ELDC's top accountant to look after the restaurant books. Katie looked after the day-to-day bookkeeping, but a woman named Christine Phim would take care of the bigger, more complicated things. The day before they'd opened, Ric even sent Christine over for a morning to make sure Katie had everything set up on the computer properly.

They'd been open one week and Katie was still putting in fifteen hour days. She was there for breakfast, handling it by herself. At eleven, Jenna and Karen showed up, and they prepared for the lunch rush.

At two, when things calmed down, she disappeared in the office to do business, re-emerging at four-thirty to get cooking for the supper crowd. She'd anticipated correctly—their supper volume was much less than lunch. After they closed at eight, she did up the deposit while the other girls cleaned up and prepared for morning. Soon she would leave the dinner hours to Jenna and Karen, and she'd be able to cut back her workload a bit. And she had to hire more help. Even though they were closed on Sundays, Jenna and Karen couldn't be expected to work six days a week. She'd asked them for recommendations of suitable people, and had set up four interviews for this afternoon.

She was in the middle of putting up two take-out orders, placing them in two Styrofoam take-away containers and adding Caesar salad to the side, when she discovered Ric's eyes watching her warmly.

Her lips curved up in welcome as she slid the containers over the counter to her patrons. They murmured their thanks and departed. She stepped back, allowing Ric to come behind the counter through the pass-through. "What are you doing here? Aren't you busy running an empire?"

He grinned. "You're in a good mood. Business seems to be brisk."

"It is. We may actually turn a profit." She spun to retrieve a meal-sized salad from the refrigerator behind her, handed it to Karen.

"I thought I'd check up on you—in person." He was out of his suit today, dressed in khaki cotton pants and a white golf shirt. The shirt set off the darkness of his tan and the sleek black of his hair, and her stomach started the queer fluttering that happened every time he was near. Staring up at him, she had a fleeting memory of his hand on her arm as they stood in her steamy bathroom, bathed in candlelight.

"Katie? I need the next pan of risotto." Jenna's voice interrupted and Katie turned away from Ric, embarrassed to be caught so obviously distracted.

"Sure. I'm on it," she replied, leaving Ric standing awkwardly in the middle of the work area.

When she came back, he was handing a bottle of iced tea to a patron. "What are you doing?"

"Helping, what does it look like?"

Jenna removed the old steel pan of rice and chicken and took it to the back while Katie slid the new one over the steaming water to keep it hot. "You don't have to do that."

"You've got them lined up to the door," Ric pointed out, and sure enough, when Katie looked up, the last person in line was holding the door open.

"Well, all right. Have you worked in a restaurant before?"

At the shake of his head, she scanned the busy dining area. "Do you think you can you work the tables? There's a dishpan for dirty dishes, a cloth for wiping and make sure the napkins and condiments are filled."

He gave her a smart salute, grabbed a plain white waitress apron from beneath the counter, and took the dishpan from Karen's hands, leaving her free to take orders and run the register.

Katie watched him out of the corner of her eye as she put up orders. He was doing well, for a corporate executive. And the apron tied around his slim hips only added to his masculinity instead of detracting from it. Her intention to keep Ric at arm's distance wasn't working very well today, and she hoped he didn't make a habit of coming in with the idea of helping. It sure didn't help her resolve at all.

He loaded dishes, took the cloth from the pocket of the apron and wiped the table clean, organized the salt and peppers and napkins neatly, and moved on to the next table. Someone had left a tip and she laughed to herself as he held the coins in his hands, debating, then put them in the apron pocket. The millionaire cashing in on a two-dollar tip.

With Karen dedicated to taking orders and running the cash, things ticked along like a good watch and the line was under control. She hadn't envisioned Ric being a hands-on sort of partner, and seeing him working around their restaurant made her realize how much their lives were intertwined.

Her hands moved automatically to fill the next styrofoam takeout container. If she wanted to keep her distance, it would be better if she kept the day-to-day running of the Pick and Choose to herself and let Ric focus on the administration. That had been their agreement, after all. She frowned as he chatted to a customer, smiling and laughing. Too irresistible by far. She turned her attention to the orders flooding her way, determined to keep her mind off Ric.

When she looked up again, Jenna was putting up the last order and the clock said one-twenty. The worst of the rush was over; traffic would be lighter now. Wiping her hands on her apron, she spied Ric at a table. He had six napkin holders in front of him and a paper-bound stack of napkins to his right. The man was a multimillionaire with a successful land company, yet he seemed content to stuff napkins into metal holders. Her respect for him grew even through her personal misgivings of having him close.

She filled a plate with risotto and Caesar and grabbed a bottle of water. Reaching his table, she put it down as he finished the last napkin holder. "The pay kind of sucks, but the fringe benefits are good."

He smiled at her then and pulled the plate closer. "I've been smelling your risotto for over an hour. I hope it tastes as good."

Katie took the holders and placed them on the tables, and when she turned back, Jenna was handing her a plate. "You need to eat too. Go keep your partner company."

Katie took it with gratitude. She'd grabbed a piece of fruit mid-morning while starting the lunch prep, and she was famished. "Thanks. Make sure you grab something too."

Ric saw her take the plate and hoped it meant she was going to join him. He'd watched her working. Her hands flew as she put up orders. The food was fresh and hot, salads crisp and cool, and she smiled easily at each and every customer. She had been right all along. She could do this, and she was darn good at it. The business she could learn. The way she cooked, offered service—that was her niche. She'd taken her friendly, outgoing personality from her youth and added a maturity to it, and he was quite taken with the result.

Katie sat across from Ric and dipped into her food. "Thanks for your help today. It was crazy and having an extra pair of hands was great."

"I'm very pleased it's so busy. The risotto is great, by the way." He chewed another forkful and leaned back in his chair. He'd never cleared tables before, or filled salt shakers. Summers he'd worked at the golf course, during the year he'd done some campus policing for spare cash. He wasn't sure he'd want to bus tables every day, but it had almost been fun. He certainly didn't think Katie needed to carry all the burden of day to day operations…and helping out kept him close to her.

"I'm a partner, don't forget that, Katie. I can't be here all the time but I don't mind helping out when I can."

"You've done too much already," she murmured, her eyes focused on her plate. "I never intended to pull you away from your own business."

He sighed, frustrated.

"God, Katie, I'm not doing you any favours, you know. I wanted a partnership because I wanted to be involved," he replied, his tone clipped with impatience. Never mind the fact he could take every opportunity to make her see how good they could be together. He softened his voice. "I don't expect you to do everything."

106

"You've provided me with your lawyer and accountant," she reminded him. "That's a big thing, too."

"I've provided *us* with Mark and Christine, because it made sense."

"Still..."

"Why are you determined not to accept help from me?" He put down his water bottle and leaned forward, resting his elbows on the table. "Don't you think I can see how hard you're working? I know how many hours it takes to start up a business. We open at seven, and I bet you're here well before that. And you're here until closing, aren't you? There's no time for anything but work for the first while. There are kinks to iron out. When was the last time you did something for fun?"

She chuckled. "I don't remember, unless you call painting and shopping for equipment 'fun'."

"You see? Let me help when I can. And for God's sake, eat. You're becoming skin and bones."

She blushed at his criticism, but he continued on. He missed her lush curves, to be honest.

"You're running a restaurant focused on good health. Doctors do make the worst patients, don't they?"

"I promise I'll eat better." She sounded like a disciplined child and his lips quirked at her petulant tone.

"I'm going to hold you to it. Even if I have to come in and make sure you do." He stacked his plate and took hers too. "This is the end of my bus-boy duty for today. I have a meeting at two-thirty, and I can't be late."

"Why didn't you say something?" She rose and took the dishes out of his hands. "I could have gotten you lunch to go, or..."

"Relax. I just don't want to lose my tee time."

He knew she realized he was teasing because her lips pursed up with annoyance and he laughed outright at her expression. "Big deal coming up. Best done over eighteen holes. I'll let him win, naturally."

"Naturally."

Conspiratorially, he leaned over and whispered, "Figuring out your opponent and what they want is the key. You can find the best way to give them what they want, while ultimately getting what you want."

He walked away, but at the door turned for a final goodbye. She pressed her fingers to her lips and giggled.

"Um, Ric?" She stared pointedly at his midsection. "You might want to leave the apron here."

He looked down, blushing as he realized he was still wearing the white apron. While he untied it, she teased him further, following him to the open door.

"Oh, and that tip you got might come in handy when you get your clubs cleaned."

Her smile was wide and he caught a glimpse of the old, carefree Katie he'd been missing.

He folded the apron, leaving the tip inside, and put it in her hands. "See you tomorrow," he murmured in her ear, treating her to an outrageous wink as he swung out the door.

Chapter Eight

It was time for stage two.

Ric pushed back from his desk and checked his watch. Eleven thirty-two. He had time to head over to the restaurant, pitch in for an hour or so, then hit her with the invitation when her guard was down.

For the past two weeks, he'd popped into the Pick and Choose several times. He'd taken a client there for lunch, had picked up dinner for himself another night, had shown up during the lunch rush and bussed tables again. Karen had even shown him how to use the register. He now had his own apron beneath the counter.

Because of this effort, he knew Katie was beginning to realize he was as committed to the day-to-day operations of their venture as she was. She was also relaxing around him more. It was in the way she held her body, the easy way her smile lit up her face when he came in the door. Less rigid and more welcoming...even, dare he think it...happy to see him.

He jogged down the stairs to the bottom floor of the building, walking out into the bright August sunshine, anticipating seeing her again today. Stepping inside the restaurant was the best part of his day, the one time where everything felt right. Every time he walked through the door, her customary smile of greeting warmed him to his toes. His steps quickened as he turned a corner, getting closer to the woman who consumed his thoughts more than he cared to admit. He frowned slightly, feeling the heat rise up from the concrete sidewalk. He had to be smarter than that. He couldn't expect everything to blithely go his way simply because he wanted it to. It's not like he'd spent the last decade pining over her. But she was here now, and he could at least admit to himself that he'd had a thing for her then, and he cared even more for her now.

Katie mustn't know how completely he was invested. She'd surely run. But he'd take his time, make her care for him the way he cared about her. It wasn't very unlike finessing a client to coming around to his way of thinking. He stopped with his fingers on the handle of the door. The big difference, of course, was that if a client went the other way, Ric was only out money. If Katie walked away, she'd take something far more valuable with her. Despite her intentions, they were emotionally involved. And he was kidding himself if he thought everything would fall into place according to his schedule.

He opened the door, and the ray of sunshine greeted him again.

"You're just in time," she called, slapping a slice of twelve grain bread on a turkey sandwich, sliding a knife through it, cutting it into two triangles, and snapping it into a plastic container. She handed it to the waiting customer and her grin flashed like lightning. "We're busier than a one-armed paper hanger. Grab an apron and pitch in."

He angled her an amused look, raising an eyebrow as he wrapped the ties around his hips. "You're unusually happy today."

"We had our best sales day ever yesterday. The new girl is working out fabulously. I got eight uninterrupted hours of sleep last night."

"Wow, three for three," Ric replied, grabbing his dishpan and lifting the pass-through. He hit the first table with a smile. His timing couldn't be more perfect.

The hour flew by. Ric cleaned tables, refilled what was low and loaded and ran the dishwasher. He restocked the take-out supplies from beneath the counter. Karen ran to the washroom; he took over taking orders and running the cash seamlessly.

Land deals were exciting, housing projects awesome to see develop, but these days nothing gave him as much pleasure as the hands-on work here at the Pick and Choose. It filled him with such a simple sense of accomplishment, something he hadn't truly felt since the first days of starting ELDC. He was starting to realize his enjoyment came from building the business, not simply running a successful one. Getting his hands dirty and watching a venture grow.

The rush tempered, then dwindled. Katie was busily jotting notes, what needed to be ordered and what to increase and decrease to balance food stocks. Ric unwrapped his apron and folded it neatly.

"What do you have planned for Sunday?" he asked.

Katie's head snapped up, and for the first time, Ric saw her expression grow guarded. He would have to be very careful and play this just right.

"Nothing. Rest."

"How about brunch?" He made his motions deliberately casual, tucking his apron in the usual place and helping himself to a drink from the cooler. He popped the top off a bottle of raspberry lemonade and leaned his hips against the Formica counter top. "Mom and Dad are having their anniversary thing this weekend. Dad's making his famous corn fritters."

"I…I don't know."

"Come on, it's only brunch," he cajoled lightly. "Your parents are coming, and I know Mom and Dad would love to see you. They haven't in years, and they know we're in this venture together."

111

He could tell she wanted to refuse but didn't know how. "I can pick you up at ten. There's brunch and presents and cake. Besides, I always get a little grief when I come to these things alone. You'd be doing me a big favour."

"I suppose I could come." Her voice was reluctant and she refused to meet his eyes.

Relief flooded him as she capitulated. If she reconnected with his family, perhaps it would help her see how connected they too could be. "And I promise you won't have to cook. Mom's already wrangled me into manning the omelette station."

Katie looked up, her eyes soft with wistful nostalgia. "It will be nice to see them again." Her smile teased a little. "Your cooking I'm not too sure of."

"They always liked you, you know. They've heard so much about you since we started the restaurant, they'll probably talk your head off."

Katie raised her hand, fluttering her list a little. "I've got to get back to the office for a while. But I guess I'll see you Sunday."

She patted his arm gently as she passed by; it burned from the touch.

"Oh, you definitely will," he murmured to himself, sticking his empty bottle in the recycle bin, a hopeful smile playing on his lips.

She didn't even realize it, but she'd essentially agreed to the next step of his plan—involvement with the family.

80 03

Katie changed clothes four times before finally settling on a feminine, flowing tank-style dress in white with a light pattern of pink and blue flowers. She slipped her feet into white open-toed pumps. In the bathroom, she fussed with her hairstyle again. Nothing seemed right, and she cursed herself quietly for being nervous about a simple brunch. She'd attended several at the Emerson home in the past, why was this one any different?

Because she was falling for Ric, that was why. And that changed everything.

She pulled the sides of her hair back and fastened them with a simple gold clip, leaving the rest to flow over her shoulders. She was uncertain about seeing his parents again. The last time she'd seen them was right after graduation. They had to know she'd rejected their son once before. Their families had run in the same circles, yet after their fallout, Katie made a point of never attending any of the same functions, even though she and Ric had always suffered through the gatherings together. What would they think of her now? Did they think she was after his money? Using him for her business? Romantically involved?

Or, heaven forbid, all of the above?

Chewing her lip, she considered changing her jewelry when the security buzzer rang, causing her to jump.

Well, there was no time now. She turned away from the mirror and grabbed her purse. She'd have to do, just as she was.

She opened the lobby door and stopped, staring at Ric.

Heart-stoppingly gorgeous. In casual khaki pants and a light blue tailored shirt, untucked, he looked like a magazine ad for casual wear. It wasn't fair for him to look so very handsome when she was trying terribly hard to keep things platonic between them. It wasn't right that, by looking down at her, he made her breath catch and her pulse flutter when she was determined to focus on the business.

"Hi," she said, the word coming out strangled as she stared at him. Every nerve ending in her body came alive the moment his lips curved up.

"You look beautiful."

And his simple words made her feel beautiful. Ric held out a hand and she took it, feeling the jolt of the contact clear up her arm and into her core. Holding hands, for Pete's sake! It was so junior high, and she hadn't realized she could still have such complicated feelings over a simple gesture. But nothing about Ric was simple…not their past, nor their current relationship, nor her feelings for him or their situation.

He led her to his car and she realized abruptly that in the months since they'd reconnected, she'd never driven with him. It hadn't been intentional, but they'd never actually gone anywhere together. It added to the feeling that this was a date, and Katie was already uncomfortable with that impression.

The car suited the man, she thought, as he opened her door and closed it after she slid her ankles inside. It wasn't flashy. At first glance, it was a nice black sedan. Yet it was more. It was classy and elegant, with soft leather interior and rich details. Ric turned the key and the engine hummed to life. This was no granny's car, Katie realized as they turned out of the lot and headed for highway. This car had more power than Ric needed. It was a stealthy machine in a conservative wrapping. She thought briefly of Ric's bedroom and the opulent décor, wondering if he was the same…a sleek cat beneath his perfect executive exterior. Now here she was, stuck in an enclosed area, so close to him the scent of his cologne tickled her nostrils and she had no means of escape.

There was more to Ric Emerson than she'd ever realized, and she could not remain immune to the implications of that.

"Mom's happy you're coming," his voice broke into her thoughts.

"I haven't seen her in years," Katie replied, glad of the distraction, turning her gaze from the window to his face. "Has she changed?"

"Not a bit." Ric's crooked smile was affectionate. "She still pretends to run the roost, but really she just dotes on Dad. And she's still terrifyingly efficient."

Katie laughed. Carole Emerson's parties always ran like clockwork. Perfectly timed, a masterpiece of organization and planning. Despite her gruff manner, Katie had always liked her. She knew a heart of gold lay beneath her brisk exterior.

"I remember your sixteenth birthday." Katie laughed at Ric's rueful expression. "It was a lovely dinner party."

"She invited a half dozen people I hardly knew and made us play croquet on the lawn."

Katie snickered. "Now come on. It was fun. We had a lovely meal and pink lemonade."

"Bah! Pink lemonade for a teenage boy's party." His lip curled as he put on his turn signal and turned into an exit, heading west.

"A cooler of beer probably would have been more popular."

Ric looked over, his face scrunched with annoyance. She laughed out loud, knowing he was half annoyed at the memory and half at her clear enjoyment of his discomfort.

"It doesn't matter. They were kids of friends of my parents. I didn't have many friends."

Katie's face sobered. Ric had been lonely as a boy. Looking at him now made it easy to forget. He was handsome, successful, at ease.

"How did you do it? How did you change so much?"

He looked away from her and his lips thinned. She waited.

After several seconds, he answered, still staring at the road straight ahead. "Sheer force of will. I learned if I wanted something only I could make it happen."

"It's amazing, you know."

He turned back to her again as they stopped at a traffic light. "You think so?"

"Absolutely."

"Hmm." He ignored the light and he looked at her as if trying to sort a puzzle. "You'd be surprised. I'm really not that different."

Katie didn't laugh. She saw he was deadly serious and she wasn't sure what to say. She'd been involved with changing her own image and she'd never considered the personal implications of Ric's own transformation.

The car started forward and Katie stared over at his profile. "If you're not different, then you're doing a damned good impression."

He didn't answer.

He wasn't the only one acting. Katie leaned back in her seat and contemplated her own transformation. On the outside, she seemed confident. At the restaurant she certainly looked like she knew what she was doing. The daily register tapes said the Pick and Choose was well on its way to success. Yet deep down, she was still terrified of failing. Still trying to break free from the perception that she wasn't made of substantial stuff.

Outside, she was a budding entrepreneur.

Inside, she was a scared girl who felt constantly out of her league. Like she was playing and imagining she was Entrepreneur Barbie, Ken by her side and at any moment she'd be called back to reality—*no, Katie, you're not that girl. What were you thinking?*

As Ric turned into the driveway of the family home, her discomfort doubled.

Her parents were coming. His parents were here. She and Ric were business partners.

But this was a date, and she knew it. They could swear it was all business until they were blue in the face, but she knew every time she looked into his eyes he had feelings for her, as she did for him. And it terrified her.

Ric led her to the side of the house and through an iron gate, heading towards the backyard. Katie heard voices talking and laughing, and her stomach tumbled. She desperately hoped people didn't automatically assume they were a couple. She hadn't gone through everything to catch a man. She'd done it to prove she could stand on her own two feet.

She wasn't sure how she could tactfully explain things without it reflecting negatively on Ric. They turned the corner into the garden and she pasted a smile on her face. Ric looked down at her briefly and gave her hand a squeeze of reassurance. "Relax," he whispered, leading her first of all to his parents.

They were standing beneath a lovely fabric gazebo. Carole was pouring champagne into a punch bowl of orange juice and Bill dropped dollar-sized amounts of batter on an electric skillet, frying up his signature fritters.

"Watch your step," Ric warned, as Katie stepped over a white extension cord. *You have no idea*, she thought, feeling her hands start to sweat and wiping them as inconspicuously as possible on the skirt of her dress.

"Morning Mom, Dad."

Carole looked up. "Ric! We were starting to wonder if you were coming!" She stepped forward, up on tiptoes to kiss Ric's cheek. She turned to Katie. "I'm glad you could join us, Katie. It's been too long since you were here."

"Happy anniversary," Katie smiled weakly, and Carole folded her in a quick hug.

"Thank you, dear." Carole released Katie and stood back, appraising. "When Ric said he was bringing you, we were so happy," she beamed.

"Mother." Ric's voice was a low warning.

Katie forced herself to continue smiling, but Carole's greeting left her uncomfortable. It seemed his mother did consider them a couple…and with Ric's quiet admonishment, he'd obviously warned her to stay away from the topic.

His warning didn't seem to fizz Carole, however. "Now." Carole clapped her hands together. "Who wants a mimosa?"

"Count me in," Katie replied tightly. She was going to need it to get through the rest of the morning.

Carole hadn't changed. She had a little more grey in her hair, and a few more crinkles around her eyes, but she was still brisk and energetic. Her white slacks were casual but expensive, paired with a summer sweater in pink and white. For a moment, Katie felt transported back in time, when she'd attended a similar brunch her senior year, in honour of Ric's graduation. Carole had made more of their relationship that day, too.

Carole put a champagne glass in her hand. "Your mother and father aren't here yet. Let me introduce you around. Ric," she said to her son. "There are platters of fruit and pastries inside. Be a dear and bring them out, please."

Katie paused, the glass half-way to her lips. "I can help him." She'd rather be helpful than social at this point. It would save answering awkward questions.

Carole pooh-poohed the suggestion. "Nonsense. You're here to enjoy yourself." She guided Katie past the griddle. "Bill, look who's here."

Ric's father came around front and winked at her. "Ah, Katie my love. Haven't you grown up." He gave her a quick hug. "How's business?"

Katie let out a breath of relief. Bill was as charming as ever, an older version of Ric, his curly hair grey and his brown eyes twinkling down at her. "Business is busy, thankfully," she laughed. "I wouldn't have it any other way."

"Good for you," he congratulated. He gestured towards her glass. "You should enjoy a few of those. Days off are rare and we must make the most of them. Now, I must get back to my fritters before I burn the batch and Carole gets on my case for not paying attention."

Carole gave her husband a mock slap on the arm and took Katie away again. She introduced Katie to the Jacobs', and Katie's was grateful that she was introduced as "family friend and Ric's business partner in a downtown restaurant". Whatever her personal feelings on the matter, Carole obviously heeded her son's warning and Katie started to relax.

Imelda Jacobs was beginning to ask some uncomfortable questions about Katie's partnership with Ric, the wink-wink-nudge-nudge kind, when familiar voices reached her ears and she smiled. "Excuse me," she offered politely, and detached herself from the conversation to meet her parents.

"Mom, Dad," she greeted happily, and went forward to give them each a hug and kiss.

Sandy Buick embraced her daughter, then handed her over to her father. "It's a shame we have to see you at a social gathering, honey," she chided. "You haven't been over for weeks. Are you sure you're not working too hard?"

Katie smiled. "Not at all. I love it." She drew back from her father's arms. "It takes a while to get a new business off the ground."

Mick beamed his approval at her. "You've done us proud, Katie," he said, and Katie felt a small niggle of resentment at the tone of surprise in his voice. When she'd planned the venture, her parents had supported her but in a patronizing, indulgent sort of way. Part of why she was doing this was to prove something to them, too.

"Well, you certainly look well," Sandy approved, touching the wide strap of Katie's dress. She peered into her daughter's eyes knowingly. "Does it have anything to do with your handsome business partner?"

"It's the champagne." Ric's voice intruded as he passed behind her, his hands filled with a huge platter of fresh fruit. Katie wanted to sink through the manicured grass into oblivion. God, had he heard her mother's last comment? Her parents laughed, but when they looked back at Katie their looks grew knowing.

"So am I right?" her mother folded her hands, confident in her assumption.

Katie pulled back. "You're wrong, Mother. Ric's my business partner, and a friend. That's all."

"Well, whatever you say, darling," Sandy answered, but her tone clearly said she wasn't convinced.

"Excuse me, but I'm going to see if Carole needs any help," Katie made excuse and disappeared before they could say more about her and Ric.

The meal was lovely. Small tables were interspersed on the lawn, their white linens brilliant in the summer sun. A small bouquet of fresh flowers from Carole's garden decorated each top. Restless, Katie wandered around the cooking area, watching Ric chat and laugh with family friends as he cooked.

"You're quite good at that," she commented as he masterfully flipped an omelette.

"High praise indeed, coming from the chef," he teased back.

"Perhaps I should take over bussing tables and you can cook." She grabbed a plate and tried to decide what she'd like in her own.

"Not likely." He scooped butter into the pan and looked up. "So what do you want in yours?"

"Everything."

"Everything it is." He scooped ham and vegetables into the butter, sautéing them lightly, adding the egg batter at just the right moment. "Things going okay?"

She smiled up at him and her heart thumped as she saw genuine concern on his face. "Despite the curious looks and impertinent comments? I'm fine," she answered.

"Sorry about that."

"Are you?" She aimed a sharp look at him, while he maintained an innocent expression.

"Of course. I wanted you to be comfortable here. Cheddar or marble?" His hand poised over the bowls of shredded cheese.

"Marble, please." She frowned at him as he added the cheese, slid the spatula beneath the egg and folded it, the golden brown bottom

121

now on the top. "Why don't I believe you? Why do I think you did this to put me on the spot?"

Ric's brows snapped together. "Lighten up, Kate. Do you seriously think I'd do something like this to torture you? Our families used to socialize quite a bit. I thought it would be nice if you were included. It would probably seem odder if you weren't here." He sounded annoyed and a little hurt, and she shrunk beneath his chastisement.

"I'm sorry. I guess I'm a little sensitive."

His gaze warmed again, to her relief. She didn't like feeling like she was in Ric's bad graces.

"You're forgiven," he said, slipping the omelette on her plate. "Make sure you grab some of Dad's fritters. He'll be hurt if you don't."

She started to walk away when he called her back. "Katie? I am sorry about the speculation. And I'm awfully glad you came."

She didn't know what to say, so she moved on to the next table to collect her fritters.

Ric finally had a chance to eat, and when the breakfast dishes were removed, Bill and Carole opened the few presents on the gift table. Ric gave them a beautifully framed picture of the three of them years earlier, when he was a young boy and they had vacationed in British Columbia. The sentimental gift earned him a kiss from his mother. One by one, the gifts were opened until only her card remained.

Katie hadn't had any money for expensive gifts; neither did she know what to get a couple on their thirtieth anniversary, let alone a couple she hadn't seen in ten years. Now next to the others, her gift seemed small and insignificant, and her face flamed.

"From Katie," Carole said, loud enough that everyone could hear, and Katie wanted to evaporate. A personal gift made it look like she and Ric were close; she didn't know how to explain their relationship was only business without it looking like she was spurning him yet again. Yet somehow it felt like lying, because her feelings for Ric were growing stronger and she needed to fight harder against them.

"Dear Carole and Bill," Carole read aloud. "This card entitles you to a private dinner at the Pick and Choose, any Sunday of your choice."

God bless her, Carole seemed to understand as she smiled warmly at Katie. "Thank you, dear," she said. "A restaurant all to ourselves, imagine! We've never done that before."

Ric stared at Katie with surprise and approval. He never expected her to bring a gift, but she had given the best thing she could. And his mother had sensed it and made it seem very special. For all her faults, he could count on Mum. As his parents posed to cut the cake, he met Katie's eyes and sensed her relief.

He was on his way to take her a piece of the cake when he was waylaid by Katie's mother.

"Ric! It's so nice to see you."

He pressed a small kiss on the cheek she presented. "You too, Mrs. Buick," he answered politely. The comments she'd made earlier about the two of them, he'd tried to joke about. There was enough atmosphere between him and Katie already, without their mothers pressuring. But what came out of the woman's mouth next surprised the hell out of him.

"It was nice of you to take Katie under your wing." She smiled her most indulgent smile. "I didn't think she'd make a go of it."

The plate with the cake suddenly seemed very heavy. This, then, was what Katie was fighting against. "Why?" His brows furrowed as he stared at her. "It was a brilliant idea backed by solid research. I'd be silly not to be a part of it."

Mick approached, putting an arm around his wife's waist. "Hello, Ric." He nodded down at the two plates Ric held. "That for Katie?"

"It is, yes." Hopefully now the comments would stop and he could escape to enjoy the sweet with his partner.

"Surprised the dickens out of me when Katie said you'd agreed to back her. She's lucky to have you. You've really made her little project a success." Mick smiled, not even aware at how much his words gave offense.

Ric saw a movement out of the corner of his eye. Turning, he saw Katie not ten feet away, within hearing of the conversation. Her eyes were glassy, face fallen in dismay. For Pete's sake, couldn't she even get a break from her own parents? He felt indignation rush through him on her behalf. These people had no idea how hard Katie had worked to get the Pick and Choose up and running.

"Opening a restaurant and running it single-handedly isn't what I'd call a 'little project'. The Pick and Choose is innovative and successful simply because Katie made it so. I'm just the financing. Did you know Katie's been putting in fourteen and fifteen hour days? She deserves all the credit."

Sandy's mouth dropped open at Ric's chastising tone while Mick simply fell silent.

"Now, if you'll excuse me," he said quietly. Katie had moved, sitting at a nearby table and staring straight ahead while going through the motions of sipping lemonade. He went to her side with the slice of cake.

"That was very nice, what you gave to my parents," he said as he placed the plate on the table beside them. He pulled out a chair and took the seat next to her.

She tried a smile but knew it fell flat. "I didn't know what to give. Next to everything else, it doesn't seem like much."

"You are too hard on yourself."

"Not nearly. I'm not the only one who thinks that way, as you recently heard."

Ric put down his fork. "That was complete garbage. 'Little project' my...well, you know what I mean. I know what it takes to get a business off the ground, and now you do, too. I think we can both agree it isn't exactly a hobby."

"They think I'll get tired of it and adopt another idea...they don't think I'll stick with this. I'm still not sure it can last."

"What happened to you, Katie? You used to be the most confident girl I knew. Carefree and fun."

"So now I'm not fun?"

"No, actually, you're not. Sometimes you forget about all the other stuff and you smile like the Katie I used to know. Like that night with the paint. But those times are too few and far between." He leaned back in his chair while she sat ramrod straight, her expression defensive. "You never seem to think what you do is good enough. Like you never quite measure up."

"That's what I'm trying to change!"

She attempted to put a bite of cake in her mouth, but put the fork back down, the morsel untasted. "Don't you see? The Katie that never took anything seriously was the fun Katie. That girl is gone."

"I miss her. And I know she's in there. Letting her come out to play once in a while doesn't mean you can't do what you've set out to do."

Her chest seemed to fill with air, making it hard to breathe. All her adult life, she'd tried to change who she was. Now Ric was here telling her he missed that person, and it was a balm to her soul. It was as if magically that carefree girl had some worth and it made her want to do better, to balance things better. If only they weren't partners...

"This is my one chance to prove I'm not a complete waste of time."

He leaned forward and, ignoring the crowd around them, took her hand. "Katie Buick," he said firmly. "You have never been a waste of anyone's time."

Tears filled her eyes and she blinked. God, the last thing she needed right now was for him to be kind, while she was trying to push him away.

"Least of all, mine," he added.

She pushed her chair back. "I...sorry...please excuse me," she stammered, and fled across the lawn.

Chapter Nine

Well, he'd botched that well. Angry with himself, he pushed the plate of cake aside roughly.

"Go after her," a soft voice said from behind him and he turned. His mother looked down at him with tender eyes. "She needs you, Ric. She hasn't failed, and you can't fail her."

Ric stared at his mom a long time, pondering the implications of what she said.

"She's hurt me before. Besides, we're only partners."

With a tearful chuckle, his mother put her hand on his shoulder. "Even you don't believe that. Go after her."

Only his mother knew what had happened that day in high school, and knew why Katie never came to any of the social functions afterward. Ric had also confided in her about how hard Katie had worked to prove herself and their business. "Okay," he murmured, and giving her arm a squeeze, set off in pursuit.

Ric turned the corner of the hedge and stopped in his tracks.

Katie stood about ten feet from the fountain, her head bowed. Even from behind, he sensed her dejection so clearly his heart ached for her. He certainly hadn't intended to make her feel worse, but somehow he had. If nothing else, he had to apologize for it.

"Katie?"

Her head lifted but she didn't turn to face him. "What?"

He moved forward, his steps silent in the rich green grass beneath his feet. "I never intended to hurt your feelings."

She cleared her throat and squared her shoulders. "You didn't."

"Then why did you run away?"

"I don't know," she answered, turning her head to the left to avoid his gaze completely.

He was at her shoulder now and gently reached out to touch it. "Sure you do. Why don't you tell me?" He turned her to face him and saw the streaks of tears on her cheeks. Oh God, he hadn't meant to make her cry. He reached out and wiped the moisture away with his thumbs.

Her breath caught at his touch and his hands stilled, the thumbs at the crest of her cheekbones. He wanted to kiss her, more than anything, but knew one kiss with Katie wouldn't be enough…and he wasn't sure she was ready.

She pulled away first, putting distance between them. "Thank you for what you said back there."

He dropped his hands and let her put some distance between them—for now. "Why would you ever think you were a waste of time?"

Katie stuck her hand out, trailing it in the trickle of water gurgling out of the small fountain. "I've never done anything important in my life. I was close once, but made a grave error in judgment."

"The job and that guy?"

He glimpsed a sad smile in profile as she dabbled in the water. "I should have known better, I suppose. I guess I was just so involved I let it cloud everything."

"You were in love with him."

"Yes. At least I thought I was, which is basically the same thing. Turns out I was a first class fool."

And the jerk had taken her trust and abused it in the worst possible way. It hadn't all been about pride then, Ric realized. It hadn't been about screwing her out of a job. Her heart had been involved, and this guy, whoever he was, his betrayal was more devastating because of it. Ric cursed the man and his underhanded methods. He had broken her heart. And that was why she found it impossible to trust her own judgment again. The pieces were starting to fit.

"It was a long time ago, Katie," he offered. "Everyone makes mistakes."

She laughed, a harsh bitter sound full of self-loathing. "Not this kind. I screwed up big time, Ric. It wasn't him. It was what I let him do to me."

Ric paused. Was she finally ready to tell him the rest of the story? He knew there was more to it, and been patiently waiting for her to trust him enough to tell it. He could ask her to confide in him, or he could wait until she offered. He flexed his fingers, mentally chiding himself for his lack of initiative. Put him in the boardroom and he was confident, commanding. Put him in front of the woman he'd adored for a third of his life and he was as unsure as he'd been the day he'd asked her to the prom. He knew very well where she was coming from. Sometimes you couldn't completely erase the person you were, no matter how hard you tried.

Katie wandered away from the fountain and towards a corner of the hedge. "I need this business to work, Ric. It means far more to me than a building and a balance sheet. It's my measuring stick."

129

He walked up to her but didn't touch her. "I know that. After high school, I was determined to succeed, to show everyone Ric Emerson knew what he was doing. I changed everything, the way I looked, what I did... It seemed to be about success and money, but it wasn't, not really. It was about validation and self-worth."

"Yes." The word came out forcefully and she laughed a little. "That's it exactly. It's about proving what's in here." She pressed a fist to her heart, then dropped it.

She straightened and turned her head away from him, but not before Ric got a glimpse of her eyes—vivid, passionate. She pointed towards a weeping birch, diverting his attention. "It's been a while since I've been here. That tree has grown. I'd forgotten about it."

He took her hand and guided her beneath the drooping branches, the tiny leaves forming a filmy curtain around them. He stood behind her, heart pumping with trepidation for what he was about to do.

"I didn't forget." His lips were close to her ear and he felt her shiver, releasing the warm scent of her perfume. "You don't remember?"

She didn't answer, and her pinkening cheeks told him she recalled the moment as clearly as he. He put his hands on her upper arms, feeling the warmth of her skin, touching her at last.

"Ten years ago at my graduation brunch. I kissed you, right here."

"I know." Her words were thick and he turned her to face him.

Katie's eyes were wide, staring up at him, bluebell-blue and beautiful and he paused, seeing uncertainty there. But he saw longing, too, and before he made the mistake of thinking too much, he cupped her face and lowered his lips to hers.

She was warm and sweet and his body coursed with joy as she responded, opening her lips. She tasted like orange and strawberry and the sharp tang of good champagne. Heart soaring, he pulled her closer so their bodies touched and he felt her soft curves flush against him. Her right hand rested on his arm, while the other slid up, twining in his curls. Still the kiss went unbroken; it grew deep and reckless and he moaned into her mouth.

The vibration of her replying groan reverberated through his head as he turned, leaning back against the trunk of the tree, the cool bark digging in through his shirt as her body pressed against him. This was the Katie he'd always imagined. Free, giving, passionate, desiring. His head spun with the taste, the scent of her, and he moved his right leg to the side, making a place to cradle her between his legs.

As they made contact, he rubbed his hips against her, letting her feel his arousal.

Abruptly she broke away and took several steps back. His lips were swollen and his mind cloudy with desire, but he clearly understood her when she gasped, "No."

"Katie," he began, running his hand through his hair with frustration. So close! They'd grown reckless and nothing had ever felt more right!

"No!" Her voice was stronger now, definite in its censure and it stopped him cold. Her feet kept stepping backward and her face was tight with distress. Eyes, wild and bright, accused him. "I can't do this," she choked out, tears streaming down her cheeks. "I told you in the beginning…business only. Why do you keep doing this to me?"

She reached the hedge and he started to move forward. He had to stop her. If nothing else he had to tell her now how he felt. If she only understood…

"Stop," she commanded.

He paused.

"This is not what I want." He saw new tears in the corners of her eyes. "No," she said again, and spinning on her heel, she ran across the grass, back to the party.

Ric leaned back against the trunk of the tree. It was probably better to let her go than chase after her and make a scene in the middle of the party. Ten years had passed and nothing had changed. What was left of his heart was shattered and laying in pieces around his feet. He'd known this could happen, he had! He knew by making a move on Katie, he was risking everything. But somehow he'd thought what they had between them transcended what had come before. Wrong. He'd trusted her enough that he'd been willing to put his heart back on the line and try again. Only it had blown up in his face.

He closed his eyes, thumping the back of his head against the tree. Hell, she'd been more gracious when they were kids. He'd kissed her then, too, but at least all she'd done is drawn back, smiled a little and said "thank you". But perhaps he should have realized she couldn't change after all. Days later, he'd asked her to the prom and the humiliation, the pain was still fresh. She'd laughed at him, and the words still taunted him.

He hadn't been good enough then, and he obviously wasn't good enough now. He saw again the accusation in her eyes before she ran. *How could you,* they'd said. She told him in the beginning their relationship had to remain professional. Oh sure, his money was good enough and he was entertaining enough as a business partner. But on a personal level, he had to remember his place. There could be no more stepping over the line like he had today.

Now she'd run back to the party and left him here. Fled like a pack of wolves was on her heels. When he returned back to the crowd, they'd all know she'd run away from him. Poor Ric, successful in business but unlucky in love. His fingers clenched, making fists. He was getting damned tired of Katie Buick making a fool of him. And he was getting tired of giving her that power.

Several minutes later, he went back to find most of the guests enjoying coffee and the bulk of the mess tidied up.

His mother spied him and hurried over. "Goodness, what happened? Katie ran back here looking like she'd seen a ghost and now you appear, looking ready to commit murder. Did you have a fight?"

"Not exactly," Ric replied tightly. "Where is she?"

"Her parents wanted to take her home, but she left in a taxi instead," Carole answered, her hand on Ric's arm. "Mick and Sandy just left."

"I see." He saw all right. He laughed, a brittle sound from deep in his throat. She was so repulsed she'd spent money out of her tight budget to get away from him as fast as she could. His kiss had been so repugnant that she couldn't wait to put space between them. He felt the eyes of his parents' friends on him, full of curiosity, some with looks of pity and he let anger take over for the pain. She'd humiliated him in public for the last time.

"Ric. Go after her."

He turned hostile eyes on his mother and she stepped away. "I did. Now I'm done chasing after Katie Buick. Done, for good."

He spun on his heel and stalked out of the party. What Katie needed was a taste of her own medicine. Someone to reject her as soundly as she'd rejected him. And he was going to be the one to do it.

§ ℃

Katie arrived at the Pick and Choose, paid the cab driver and went inside, locking the door behind her.

The restaurant looked different in the dim afternoon light. The striped awnings held out most of the sun, casting a dismal shadow over the silent counter. It was quiet, eerily so, with no hiss of the grill or clicking of the cash register. No customers chatted, no bell dinged as the door opened and shut in the noon rush. The only sound was the quiet hum of the drink cooler. For the moment, the restaurant was completely hers, and she should have taken joy in the possession of it. But Ric's kiss coloured everything, making all aspects of her life more complicated.

She went to the fridge, took out a bottle of water, and pulled up a chair with a screech of iron on tile.

If Ric wanted to talk, he'd assume she'd go home. And she was determined not to be there. There was nothing for them to talk about.

"Nothing!" She shouted at the empty restaurant, taking a belligerent swig of water. There was nothing to talk about, because nothing was going to happen between them ever again. It couldn't.

Her lips still tingled from the warm taste of him. His voice in her ear had sent shivers through her body, and a longing so strong she'd been incapable of stopping him from kissing her. When he'd touched his lips to hers, pulled her close, she'd responded like she'd wanted to for weeks, all the reasons why she shouldn't fleeing her mind on the summer breeze. He'd moaned in her mouth, pressed his hips against hers, and she'd snapped back to reality. This was all wrong for her and she couldn't, wouldn't, let it go on and lose sight of the goal. There were things more important than fun...and fooling around with Ric was a chance she wasn't willing to take. It had the potential of ruining their partnership and failure of what she was trying to accomplish. The business was going well, and she was darned proud of how well her hard work had paid off. But if she and Ric started a personal relationship, how much of the credit would go to him? How many would feel like her own parents did, that Ric indulged her in her "pet project"?

No, their relationship had to stop now, before it got out of hand.

She knew how it would go. She'd let herself get involved with him and for a while, things would be great. Undoubtedly they'd sleep together. The thought made her body flush and she forced her thoughts to move on. But after a few weeks, maybe a month, he'd get bored. She wouldn't be smart enough to hold his interest, or entertaining enough for his friends. Things would get awkward, and he'd politely let her down easy, with a standard line like "we're better as friends" or "you're a great person, I'm just not ready for this kind of relationship right now". She'd heard the excuses before, those and a dozen more.

She'd never been able to hold a relationship any better than she'd held a job. Part of that, she knew, was because she'd never been satisfied, never felt like she was where she belonged, like she did now. Pulling out a second chair, she slid off her shoes and put up her feet. He was making it so hard. It would be much easier to remain aloof if he had no idea how she felt.

But he did. And he was willing to give her the assurance she craved. The whole bit about never being a waste of time. She snorted. That was damned good, she had to admit. And the validation and self-worth angle—it was like he saw right into her heart! But what if she gave in and let herself become romantically involved like she wanted to? What if he took it away again? What if he discovered he didn't genuinely care for her after all? What would happen to the Pick and Choose? They were partners, but she never for a moment forgot he controlled the purse strings. He could hire someone to run it for him. She couldn't run it without his cash flow.

And how shallow did that make her? Did she only want him for his money?

She kicked the chair away in a very unladylike manner and rose, pacing the dusty floor. No, not shallow, she defended herself. From the moment she'd entered Ric's office, it had always been about the business and not about falling in love with him.

She stopped in her tracks, putting a hand to her mouth. No. No, no, no. It wasn't possible. Had the thought that she was in love with Ric really flown through her mind?

Well, wasn't this a fine kettle of fish? Her lower lip trembled as she realized she had indeed fallen, head over spatula, in love with him. Now she'd gone and screwed it up. Damn Ric and his soulful brown eyes and hard body and soft lips...lips that had only an hour before been on her own as his hands pulled her closer. And he was a much better kisser now than he'd been a decade earlier. Toe curling, scalp-tingling good. So good she hadn't wanted to stop.

Ever.

She was in love with Ric Emerson and it was the worst possible thing that could have happened. He mustn't know how she felt. Because she would not break the vow she'd made to herself.

The Pick and Choose came first. Making it as a success came first. And she was willing to suffer whatever need be to see it through.

Even her heart.

$\wp$ $\wp$

Ric entered his office, tossed his yellow hard hat on a chair, and headed for his desk. He was spending more and more time on site, overseeing the latest property development in the northeast part of the city. The rest of the time he spent in his office and in meetings. Ric limited his involvement with the Pick and Choose to impersonal e-mails and correspondence with the accountant. He no longer popped in over the lunch hour to grab a bite or help out with the noon rush. He left the day-to-day running of the restaurant to Katie. That had been the original agreement and he was darn well going to abide by it.

She didn't want to see him, it was clear. After running from him at the brunch, she'd never even attempted to call him or explain. Her actions said it all. She'd pushed him away and put as much distance between them as possible; it was hard to misinterpret that as anything other than outright rejection.

He'd get back to what he did best. Making money. Clearly he wasn't cut out for personal relationships, and he was through wasting his time.

Except for one thing. He wanted to hurt her as she'd hurt him. Just once, make her feel the burning humiliation of rejection. He scowled in the small mirror he kept on the wall, the one he used to assess his appearance before walking into the boardroom. Perhaps she'd see things a little differently after a taste of her own medicine.

The method of her downfall, however, was still being elusive.

Ric opened his briefcase and took out yesterday's mail. Flipping through, he paused at one plain white envelope. The return address was to Lisa Carlton, Bishop High Reunion Committee. Curious, he sliced it open to find an invitation to his ten-year reunion, along with an agenda of events. The white paper with the red and black logo in the top corner shook in his hand. Did he even want to attend such an event? No one would recognize him, and no one would care. He'd skated through high school a social outcast, with next to no friends. There would be no one with which whom to share fond memories. He had precious few.

He tossed the sheet down on the desk, frowning at it. Moving on, he opened the rest of his mail and dealt with it, but in the end went back to the stiff stationery of the high school. He noticed a luncheon planned for the Saturday. Perhaps he could get them to cater it with the Pick and Choose. It would be good publicity.

He stared at the contact name. Lisa Carlton was chair of the Reunion Committee. Jan Grandin was the vice-chair. Both girls had been in the group who had laughed at him from behind the lockers when he asked Katie to the prom.

What would they think of him now? Would they be surprised to find a transformed, wealthy Ric? Living in such a large city ensured he hadn't crossed paths with many of his former classmates. A plan began formulating in his mind, a method of making Katie pay for hurting him so deeply. Resolutely he pushed down the heaviness of guilt he felt for setting her up. If she'd offered an explanation, even a bad attempt at an apology, perhaps it wouldn't hurt so much.

But he'd honestly thought they'd grown closer, and her clear dismissal of him proved him wrong about her again.

Before he changed his mind, he picked up the telephone and punched in seven numbers.

"Hello, Lisa? Ric Emerson speaking…yes, that Ric Emerson. Do you have a caterer for your luncheon yet? Because I've got a proposition for you…"

80 03

She'd avoided him long enough.

Katie put the finishing touches on the prep work for the evening shift and peeled off the thin plastic gloves she wore when dealing with the food. It had been two weeks. In that time, the Labour Day long weekend had come and gone, and business was regular now that summer and vacations were winding down. Last night, she'd stayed up until midnight, working the figures for July and August. She could deliver them to Christine by e-mail, or she could drop them by ELDC herself, and stop in to give Ric a progress report. Besides, he'd e-mailed about the possibility of catering a lunch at the reunion. They should discuss it and put together a proposal. She had been surprised he'd called Lisa about it. She remembered quite clearly now that Lisa and Jan had been two of the girls who had put him down the most. Truthfully, Katie wasn't looking forward to seeing them again; she couldn't imagine what would have prompted Ric to approach them.

Despite the fact they had things to discuss, Katie dreaded seeing Ric again. Beyond the most rudimentary e-mails, they hadn't spoken since the brunch. And it was going to be awkward at the very least. But she had to get it over with sometime. She washed her hands at the sink, drying her hands on the brown paper towel she kept in a stack beside the soap. What kind of business would they have if they couldn't even stand to talk to each other in person?

He deserved some sort of explanation. She'd bite off her own tongue before admitting she was in love with him, and she was sure it would pass. But he at least needed to know that her priority was the same as it always was, business—and that her stepping away was nothing personal.

The sun was rich and mellow as she stepped outside. This was her favourite time of year. Her shoes made quiet steps on the sidewalk as she shouldered her purse, gripping the brown envelope in her fingers and heading in the direction of ELDC. The concrete was sprinkled with yellow poplar leaves, already turning and falling in the shortening days, releasing the pungent smell of early autumn. Out of the corner of her eye, she spied a young couple wandering under the arches of Olympic Park, holding hands. Briefly, she wondered what it would be like to do that with Ric, to leave all the complications behind and enjoy an intimate walk with nothing to worry about but an evening chill as the sun disappeared behind the buildings of downtown.

She stepped inside ELDC's lobby and pressed a hand to her stomach. What would she say to him? How would he look, and would she want to kiss him again? Would he be angry or understanding? Cold or indifferent?

She shook her head. *Stop worrying, and do it*, she commanded herself, and headed to the elevator.

Christine was gone for the day, so Katie put the envelope on her desk, scribbling a brief message on a post-it note and tacking it to the top. She wiped her hands on her jeans, straightened the fitted T-shirt she wore and ran a hand over her ponytail. Taking several deep breaths, she headed towards the big oak door at the end of the hall.

It was open a few inches and she tapped lightly, receiving no answer. She pushed it open hesitantly, peering inside to see if Ric was there. It was quiet and still; it appeared he was gone. Stepping in, she saw his briefcase on the floor beside the desk and a suit jacket over the back of his chair.

She should leave right now, come back later when he was here, but she couldn't resist the urge to sneak in. She tiptoed across the floor as she approached the desk. She couldn't shake the feeling she was spying somehow, but she'd been two weeks without hearing his voice or seeing his face. The urge to wander through his office was too great, and she reached out her fingers and touched the thick fabric of his jacket.

The area around his desk even smelled like him; a scent she couldn't name but remembered as one distinctly his. The jacket was navy, perhaps the same one he'd worn during their first meeting. They had seen each other so much she already knew it was one of his favourite colours. She smiled, a little sadly. He'd been cold that day too, official, businesslike. That had changed as they saw more of each other. His strength, his determination, paired with the vulnerability and insecurity he'd revealed was a big part of why she loved him.

Several slips of pink paper were piled beside his phone—his phone messages, taken by his assistant. His day planner lay open on his desk and she stared at the neat writing under the date. Meetings, conference calls, bid openings. Curious, she turned the pages, marveling at how hectic his life was, yet he'd still made time for their venture. Her fingers paused as she got to next Tuesday's date.

Meeting with Lisa and Jan at P&C—aka Katie gets her comeuppance.

What on earth did that mean?

She read on, although she had to squint to read the tiny script beneath the entry. It was written, not in appointment style, but almost like a diary, which seemed odd to her.

Katie will finally learn what it is to be humiliated in public. And in front L &J— the perfect set up.

Katie's eyes blurred as the flush of anger rose up her neck and burned her ears. How dare he? Her fingers lifted off the pages as if they were on fire. He was planning on embarrassing her, in her own restaurant, in front of her clients? He was using their business as a method to bring her lower than she already was? And she'd honestly considered herself in love with this man?

Hastily, she put the book back to today's date and slung her purse over her shoulder. She'd thought he'd understood. She'd told him things she never talked about. They had become friends, and he said he understood her need to prove herself and most of the reason why she had to keep things professional. But all he really understood was his own blasted ego. So what if she'd pulled away when they'd kissed, and she hadn't elaborated as to why? She'd just realized the true depth of her feelings, for Pete's sake! And it's not like he asked her to explain. But this...this was taking things too far. It was juvenile and petty and she hadn't thought him capable of such a thing.

She rushed out of his office, blinded by angry tears. Punching the button to the elevator, she decided not to wait and pushed through the heavy door at the end of the hall, taking the stairs. So he planned to humiliate her? Well, she'd see about that!

Chapter Ten

When the lunch rush died down, Jenna cornered Katie and told her straight. "Get your purse. We're going for a walk."

Katie looked around. Sure enough, it was quiet. Only two patrons occupied a table and the bell above the door was silent. But payroll needed tending and she had a supply list she had to complete and fax. "I don't have time."

"Make time," Jenna insisted. "If you don't get out of here for a while you're going to drive us crazy. Karen will hold the fort until we get back."

With a sigh, Katie relented. Fact of the matter was, it was a gorgeous early fall day and Katie could use some sunshine. She'd been entirely too wound up about the whole Ric situation and it was starting to tell.

"Half an hour. That's it," she relented, and before she could change her mind, Jenna pulled her out the door.

"Where are we going?"

"First, we're getting you an iced coffee. With whipped cream and chocolate shavings on the top." Jenna paused outside a door. "Nope, you'd better come in with me. I can't take a chance of you taking off and going back to work."

Katie grinned. Jenna was such a breath of fresh air. No nonsense, tell it like it is, loyal to a fault. A keeper of secrets and open minded. "You know me too well," she laughed, following Jenna inside.

Minutes later, they emerged with two gigantic plastic cups, filled to the brim with mocha iced coffee and mounds of whipped cream. The sun beat down on Katie's face, warming her hair until it radiated through her to her fingertips. "This feels good," she admitted.

They stopped at Olympic Plaza and sat on a bench to watch children frolicking in the water, making the most of the last days of summer. For a few minutes they sipped, until Jenna broke the silence.

"So what happened?"

Katie stared straight ahead at the arches. She knew if she looked at Jenna, Jenna would know right away what the problem was. "I don't know what you mean."

"Stop playing dumb, Kates. This is me you're talking to. You've been miserable all week. You might as well spill it."

"I'm tired." Well, it was partly true. She was tired. She'd been putting in marathon days for weeks now.

"What happened with Ric? He's never around now. Ever since the brunch…"

Jenna paused, and Katie felt like a bug under a microscope.

"That's it, isn't it? Something happened at the brunch." She wiggled closer. "What?"

Oh, she might as well admit it. Jenna was like a dog with a bone now and would keep at her until she admitted the truth. "Yes, something happened at the brunch. He kissed me."

Jenna's straw stopped on the way to her lips. "I knew it! How was it?"

"Better than the first time," Katie admitted without thinking, colouring as Jenna hooted.

"More than once? Katie dear, you've been holdin' out on me." She angled her body sideways, eager for more information.

Katie risked a glance at Jenna and couldn't help smirking a bit. "Oh shut up. Yes, it was more than once. He kissed me one night before we even opened." Katie's insides curled at the remembrance of dancing in his arms. "But at the brunch we were under this tree and he…"

She stopped short of graphic details. "Oh, you get the picture. Anyway, I backed off. I think he's still mad."

That was the understatement of the century.

"Why would you back off? Have you looked at him lately? That body and dark looks, the way he gazes at you when he thinks no one is watching…girl, you'd be stupid to pass that up."

"I can't." Her gaze grew troubled, and she concentrated on a piece of grass between her sandals. "You know why," she said quietly.

"Because of the man whose name we dare not speak."

Katie nodded.

"Well, maybe you won't say it, but I will. Craig was swine. What he did to you was inexcusable." Jenna's normally bubbly voice took on a derisive edge. "Surely you aren't measuring Ric with *that* yardstick."

The sun went under a cloud and Katie crossed her arms. "I thought I loved Craig and I trusted him. Look how he betrayed me. I'd be stupid to take that kind of chance again."

"Are you in love with Ric?"

A boy on rollerblades zoomed by while Katie thought about her answer. "It doesn't matter," she said in the end. It didn't because she knew she'd already pushed Ric to his limit. There were only so many times a guy could try, after all.

"It does matter," Jenna replied, laying a comforting hand on her arm. "Craig treated you terribly. And yes, you worked with him. But honey, it doesn't mean Ric will do the same thing."

Losing the job Katie could have handled and recovered, but the horrible accusations had ruined any reputation she might have gained. "I can't take that chance, don't you see? I can't risk it for the restaurant. I've worked too hard to build it, and I want to keep it successful."

Jenna sniffed. "Keep telling yourself that. You're more afraid of risking your heart. Ric wouldn't use you, and you know it."

Wouldn't he? She'd hurt him enough he was already planning how to hurt her and do it publicly.

He made her pulse race and her heart ache. He kissed like the devil and defended her, even to her own parents. Perhaps that was why his planned betrayal cut her to the core. "Let it go, Jenna." She stood, tossed her empty cup in a nearby receptacle. "It's the only thing that makes sense."

ℰ℧ ℭℛ

The door opened, the bell dinging a cheery welcome. Katie checked her watch for the third time in a half hour. Eleven-thirty. She should go freshen up now. Lisa and Jan would be arriving any moment—and so would Ric. She wasn't sure she was up to dealing with him. It had been soon after realizing she loved him that she'd discovered he was out to hurt her after all. As mad as she was about it, she couldn't move past the piercing hurt that had come with that discovery.

Her lip curled as she shut the door to the staff bathroom behind her. She still couldn't quite believe he was planning to publicly humiliate her. The Ric she thought she knew wasn't capable of something so malicious, and if she weren't a bundle of nerves about today, she'd almost feel sorry for him for carrying a grudge for such a long time. He told her weeks ago that the past was the past and they didn't need to talk about it. But obviously that was a lie. If he had truly forgiven her for past transgressions, he wouldn't be planning something so low now.

She swiped on lip gloss and reapplied her mascara. She still regretted that day by her locker and now she was regretting it even more. The truth was she hadn't been as shallow as he thought. If he'd asked her earlier, she would have said yes, and the hell with what her friends thought. As it was she'd only been asked by one of the jocks the day before.

But Ric didn't know that and it would sound silly to say such a thing now. He knew what he thought he knew and was hurt enough, angry enough, to have planned to humiliate her today.

Initially, she'd wanted to pay him back. But after talking with Jenna, she realized the best course of action was to defuse the issue, trying to keep things on an even keel. She had a plan, and if it worked, it would simply take the wind out of Ric's sails and they could move on, salvaging a business relationship. She hoped.

Her reflection was unhappy as it looked back at her but at least her appearance was flawless. She was aiming for casual, and naturally, young. These were girls she hadn't seen in the ten years since graduation. They were chairing the reunion committee—and vain as it sounded, looking youthful was important.

Her faded black jeans were stylish and flattering, resting easily on her hips, and her blouse was flowing and sleeveless, the red a perfect foil for the remnants of her summer tan. She kept her makeup sheer and natural, but let her hair fall in light curves over her bare shoulders. She kept her nails trimmed and plain but her toes were painted light pink and a silver toe ring glimmered around the straps of her sandals.

Her inspection complete, she took a breath, released it, and opened the door.

Coming out, she heard the tinkle of the bell again and looked up to see Lisa and Jan enter together.

Jan had changed little. Her dark hair was pulled into a simple French braid, her brown eyes large and shy. Her figure had rounded a little, but she dressed casually in blue jeans and a light tan summer sweater. She was still quiet, unassuming Jan.

Lisa, on the other hand, wore heels to boost her five-foot-three height, and a fluttery white skirt about three inches too short. Her lime green camisole top clung to her midriff, and as she turned to examine the lunch board, the back hem slid up and Katie stared at a blue squiggly line she couldn't quite distinguish…the edge of a tattoo. For a moment, Katie smiled grimly to herself—in contrast to Jan's appropriate dress, Lisa looked slutty.

At that moment, Lisa turned from the specials board and met Katie's eyes.

"Katie!" Lisa's squeal had patrons turning their heads and Katie tried not to wince. Okay, she'd dressed youthfully but she was well beyond teenage squeals of greeting. She pasted on a welcoming smile and stepped forward, holding out a hand to avoid an embarrassing embrace. "Lisa! Jan! I'm glad you could come." The words came out less than enthusiastic and Katie tried to smile wider to make up for it.

Jan shook her hand and smiled, but Lisa ignored it and squeezed her into a too-tight hug. "God, you look the same as you did ten years ago," she gushed.

"I've saved us a table." Katie led them to a corner table for four and plucked the "reserved" label off the surface. Her gaze strayed back to the door, looking for Ric. As much as she knew in her head what he had planned for her, she couldn't help the flit of anticipation of seeing him again. She'd grown so used to seeing his face, to sharing a smile or laugh with him, that she missed it.

Lisa said something and diverted Katie's attention back to the task at hand. She must not forget Ric's purpose for today. She couldn't let her feelings make her soft.

The girls seated themselves and Katie graciously offered, "Can I get you something to drink?"

Little had changed in the intervening years. Lisa, with her high heels and highlighted blonde hair, used too much makeup to cover the beginnings of crow's feet. Paired with her clothing, the effect was one of someone trying to look like a teenager and actually looking older than she was. She still commanded attention with a natural sense of drama, and Jan seemed to follow in her wake. In high school, Lisa'd been the leader while Jan had followed behind like a worshipping puppy dog, rarely exerting her own opinions. Now, when Lisa ordered a diet soft drink, Jan did the same. Returning with the beverages, Katie took a seat beside Jan—the less intimidating of the two. At least Jan seemed to look at her with something akin to pity as Lisa babbled about anything and everything, never quite managing to sound sincere.

"So this is your restaurant," Lisa's voice tinkled as her eyes scanned the seating area. "It's a nice little spot, don't you think, Jan? So nice to see something health conscious."

Katie gritted her teeth at Lisa's emphasis on "little". Clearly, the Pick and Choose hardly was worth her notice, and Katie nearly bit her tongue trying not to say what was on her mind. *Where do you get off* came to mind, but instead she took a breath and said, "It's been fun watching it come together." Katie stared at the doorway again. Damn him for making her do this alone. "Hard work and long days, but I'm very pleased with how we're doing."

"We?" Lisa leaned in, a manicured finger resting speculatively on her chin.

"That's right," Jan broke in. "You have a business partner. Ric Emerson. We were surprised to hear from him."

"I couldn't have made this possible without Ric." She hoped her voice didn't sound as flat as she thought it did. For days now, Ric had only been involved by e-mail or telephone, and always about business technicalities. It was what she'd wanted from the beginning, but now things seemed quiet and lackluster without his impromptu appearances and help.

She folded her hands in her lap. In her mind, she saw the scrawl in his day planner, *Give Katie her comeuppance...* and she wished he'd come in. How could she care so much for someone who wanted to hurt her completely? It was something she didn't understand, but it wouldn't be the first time she'd been duped in that way. At least this time she saw it coming. And she was prepared. Now she wished he'd show up so they could get it over with, whatever happened. She only wanted to still be standing at the end of the day.

Lisa giggled, leaning forward as if sharing a secret. "Is he still as nerdy as ever? I heard he started up some company. I can't imagine. He was such a skinny little dork."

"Ric's definitely changed since high school." *Unlike you, you catty witch.* Katie was actually ashamed she'd ever considered this person her friend. It was evident at least in one way Lisa remained seventeen. She was still completely self-absorbed and immature.

"However, it appears he's running a bit late. Why don't we order some lunch, and you can see for yourself if our menu is something you'd like at your luncheon."

They placed their orders and Katie went behind the counter to fix them personally, wanting to demonstrate she was capable of running all aspects of the restaurant. Never let it be said she let others do the work for her. This was her business, from the top right on down to the smallest job. Besides, by making their meals, she avoided the endless, meaningless chit-chat.

She took special care with their food, picking the choicest ingredients and placing them to best advantage on the plates. She'd eat later, if at all. Right now she was wondering where on earth Ric could be. He'd said eleven-thirty, it was nearly twelve. He was always very punctual. Maybe he wouldn't turn up at all and leave her twisting in the wind, dealing with the women on her own. If business had come up, he surely would have called and left a message. What if he couldn't get here? What if there had been an emergency of some sort?

Stop it, you ninny, she chided herself as her hands paused over a salad. Ric was a big boy. And despite her conflicted feelings, his whereabouts weren't her concern. She told herself to stop worrying and delivered their lunch.

She was placing Jan's in front of her when the door opened and she saw him enter. Darn it, he'd worn those jeans again and the white shirt that made her mouth water. She turned away quickly from him and the sense of relief that flooded her at his appearance. She was supposed to be mad at him, not elated he was here and unhurt! She hated the fact she had to keep reminding herself of it.

The counter-plan. She had to remember it and get the ball rolling!

"So, Jan, I see you've married." She prompted the quieter of the two with an encouraging smile.

On cue, Jan fluttered her ring. "Yes, a year ago. What about you, Katie? Married? Seeing anyone?"

Knowing Ric was in hearing range, she smiled her brightest smile as Jan took the bait. "Actually, I just started seeing someone. He's amazing."

She sensed Ric behind her and straightened now that the plates were in place.

"What's he like?" Lisa picked up her fork, looked up and her gaze settled somewhere behind Katie's shoulder. Katie pretended not to notice and fairly oozed adoration.

"Oh, he's tall, dark, and definitely handsome. I'm crazy about him." Her voice was smooth as melted butter and she delivered a wink for added effect. Her smile wobbled a bit as she realized she'd actually described Ric. Why couldn't she have said he was blonde and blue eyed and cute as hell?

Because that wasn't what she wanted. She wanted Ric and now he had to go and screw everything up. She wasn't going to be the casualty this time, though.

"Good afternoon, ladies."

Ric interrupted and Katie kept smiling even though the simple sound of his voice made her heart thump ridiculously.

"Ric? Oh my God. You *have* changed!" Lisa's eyes grew wide as her voice rose with over-the-top enthusiasm.

He smiled, ignoring the shrill quality of her outburst. "Apparently I'm 'tall, dark, and definitely handsome', as well." He slid an arm around Katie's waist and she didn't know whether to melt through the floor or elbow him in his perfect abs. This was not her plan. Her plan was to make him insanely jealous—and to take any power away he might have had. If his plan had been to publicly reject her, then only he would look stupid if she already had another boyfriend.

But instead, he clued in far too quickly and decided to work it to his advantage, making them seem like a couple and stopping Katie's plan cold.

She had to stop underestimating him.

How dare he? The idea had been to stop him from humiliating her publicly. She knew very well he'd planned to come in here and reject her personally, and she'd planned to take the wind out of his sails by hitting him with the idea of a new, improved, boyfriend.

Instead he trumped her hand by pretending to "be" that boyfriend. Now...oh God....now he could make it even worse. Her stomach plummeted with dread. Now he could make it seem like she was truly over the moon for him, still break up with her, and make her look even worse than before. Why, oh why hadn't she thought of this angle?

Because she was no good at plans and subterfuge, that's why. She wore her heart on her sleeve and it made her easy pickings for men who wanted to hurt her.

"You weren't meant to hear that." She slapped his arm lightly, trying to simper while inside she was seething.

He put his lips close to her ear. "Liar," he whispered, and her resulting blush had Lisa and Jan grinning from ear to ear. She trembled, reacting to the warm breath on her ear and the fear that he'd actually accomplish what he'd set out to do today.

"So," he said, pulling away from Katie and taking the vacant seat beside Lisa. He leaned back in the chair and angled himself slightly towards the blonde who was staring at him without attempt to disguise it. "Your lunch is getting cold."

"Ric. You've turned out...well." Lisa smiled widely while Jan and Katie stared in amazement. "Gorgeous, in fact. Who would have guessed? You make a girl's mouth water."

Katie gaped. Of all the audacity. It was brash and tasteless and made Katie want to interject with *Hello, I'm standing right here!* And he was no better, staring back at her like he loved every minute of it. For all Lisa knew Ric was taken...yet she was hitting on him in plain sight. They weren't even a real couple, but Katie still felt justified in her anger.

He smiled back, his teeth flashing at her compliment. "It's Katie's food making your mouth water. Enjoy it. We can discuss the catering part later. Katie does a great job running the Pick and Choose. You can count on her to deliver, I assure you."

Oh damn, she felt humiliated already. Running the Pick and Choose? She owned it, or had he forgotten? He made her sound like a glorified manager.

She aimed a weak jab, "Ric handles the boring business part, and I handle the product. You can iron out the business details while I take care of my lunch crowd. If there's anything you'd like to sample, or questions about the service, please let me know. Ric, did you want some lunch, sweetheart?" The question came out sticky sweet and he smiled up at her like she was the sun warming his day.

"Not right now. Maybe later?"

The intention was clear—*perhaps a little one on one time, darling, when things aren't so busy?*

"Of course. We do have some business to take care of...later. Now, if you'll excuse me..."

She left them there and took her place behind the counter. The spot on her ribs where his hand had squeezed still tingled from the touch. No matter how angry she got, no matter how hard she tried to avoid him, she couldn't escape the fact she had fallen for him. She couldn't erase the memory of his kiss from her mind and couldn't stop the physical reaction he created simply by being in the same room with her.

But would he carry on with his plan? He had the perfect set up, and she couldn't be sure if he was building things up only to make the crash more spectacular, or if he'd changed tactics. Either way, she didn't like it. She was completely out of her depth and unsure, and that was a feeling she tried to avoid at all costs.

Her hands flew, putting up orders of sandwiches and wraps. Her spatula rang out as she stir-fried chicken and vegetables on the grill for a pita, and all the time she heard their voices and laughter ringing in her ears. Oh, the stupid man had won them over as well. Wasn't he Mr. Perfect now? And hadn't she given him the perfect ammunition to annihilate her in front of the girls? Oh, Lisa would enjoy that. Katie folded a wrap viciously as she remembered another woman, much like Lisa, looking down at her with derision and pity. "She's pathetic, and not worth your time, but if this is what you want to do, Craig, I'll go along with it."

The betrayal was still as fresh today as it had been two years ago. And now she was setting herself up for it all over again.

Her resentment fuelled her frustration and she chopped lettuce like a demon possessed. Ric approached, all smiles and congeniality, requesting cake for dessert. She arranged two pieces, topped them with a perfectly round scoop of frozen yogurt and garnished them with fresh raspberries.

"I'll serve them myself," she snapped, and Ric held open the pass-through for her to carry them forth. His stare penetrated through her back as she retreated. The more he became more perfect, the smaller she felt.

"Chocolate cake, as requested." She smiled her prettiest smile as she placed them on the table. *I should have been an actress*, she thought as she stepped back, putting her weight on one hip. Ric resumed his seat, watching her curiously. She ignored him. "Fat free, of course, with low fat frozen yogurt. We also have a fruit cup for dessert and a sugar free fruit crumble."

"Your food is great, Katie," Jan said, putting down her fork. She looked up at Katie almost sympathetically as Lisa not-so-subtly scooted her chair closer to Ric's.

"Yes, it's quite passable," Lisa added, her eyes challenging. Katie looked down at her, hoping she looked more confident than she felt. After all, for all Lisa knew, Ric was Katie's. She had the upper hand here, and she couldn't let herself forget it. She said nothing, just raised an eyebrow at Lisa's lukewarm comment as she smiled.

In retaliation, Lisa put a hand on Ric's arm. His head lifted sharply but Katie ignored him, focusing on Lisa instead.

"As Ric pointed out," Lisa continued, "it's only right to support one of our own graduates. Plus, as he mentioned, it's good publicity for you. If we can agree on a price, of course. We only have so much budgeted."

"I'm sure we can come to an agreement." Katie's voice was cool in response to Lisa's patronizing tone. Ric pointed out. Ric was after publicity. Wasn't he all goodwill and influence?

"I'm thinking a hot dish, perhaps a small assortment of wraps, a couple of salads, and the cake for dessert."

"That certainly sounds doable. Why don't you fax me with the items you want in particular, and we'll get it arranged."

"Here's the fax number," Ric pulled out a pen and wrote it on a napkin. Lisa stopped his progress with a long red fingernail on top of his hand.

"Sure you don't want to put your number on there too, Ric?" Her voice was all sweetness and innocence. "I may have questions."

Oh, Katie wanted to tan his hide as he took the moment to look deeply into Lisa's eyes and she preened beneath his gaze.

He almost looked sorry to answer, "I think Katie's the one to ask," folding the napkin in half and handing it to her.

"I'm glad you enjoyed your meal," Katie offered through clenched teeth. "Of course, it's on us." She turned her attention to Ric who was still smiling pleasantly. She wanted to wipe it off his face, yet at the same time felt some relief that it didn't seem like he was going to make a scene and dump her. "Do you have a few moments? I have something to discuss with you in the office."

"Certainly." He rose and took the time to shake both Lisa and Jan's hands, holding Lisa's a little longer than necessary. "Thanks for coming. We'll be in touch."

"You can count on it," Lisa answered, rising and looping her purse over her shoulder. Jan followed her but turned at the last moment to give Katie a quick hug. "It was good to see you again, Katie," she whispered. "Sorry about Queenie."

Katie snorted before she could help it. She'd completely forgotten about the nickname they'd had for Lisa back then. She gave Jan's hand a squeeze. "Come back anytime," she offered, and meant it.

Ric was waiting for her behind the counter. The smile dropped from her face as she breezed through the pass-through and past him to the back office.

Chapter Eleven

Katie shut the door behind them with a harder bang than was necessary, and Ric knew he was in for it. *Bring it on*, he thought acidly. Having it out with Katie was probably a good idea. They certainly needed to clear the air. Anything would be a nice change from not talking at all. He kept to the opposite side of the room, leaning back casually against a small table with steel legs, keeping his pose deliberately relaxed. They were overdue for a fight, and Ric had lots to say. In time.

"What the hell was that?"

The words were sharp, ripe with annoyance, and he attempted a flirty smile in the dim light provided only by the computer monitor.

"Jealous, darling?"

Her shoulders squared and her fists clenched at his glib response, and he chuckled, trying to infuriate her further. Goading her was the only way he knew to make her be completely honest.

"As if," she scoffed. "It's one thing to act like we're a couple. But to flirt with Lisa right under my nose? That's rude. It's demeaning to flirt with another woman in front of your girlfriend, or didn't they teach you that in graduate school?"

He narrowed his eyes as the fax machine bleeped and hummed behind him. "You're not my girlfriend, nor do you want to be, or are

159

you forgetting that small detail?" The caustic remark was laced with disgust. "And if there's nothing between us, you have no reason to be upset. Right?"

"It's not about me being jealous, you idiot. It's about you making me look like a fool!"

"So this is all about appearances, and how you look in front of other people." He nodded sagely, as if he knew exactly what she was thinking. "The hell with feelings, let's worry about what other people think!"

He clamped his mouth shut, trying abysmally to keep the fake smile in place. He realized belatedly that he had done exactly the same thing at the brunch. He'd worried not about why Katie left, but only the implications on himself. But it would be a cold day in hell before he would admit it to her.

"Don't turn this around on me, Ric. Don't you dare! You deliberately played along with that…that…well, we both know what she is. And you made me feel small and insignificant, just to embarrass me!"

The grin he'd tried to keep in place faded completely. "And what were you doing, hmm? 'Tall, dark, and definitely handsome'? Please." His nose turned up in derision. "How to make Ric look stupid, One-oh-one."

Her hands braced on her hips as she retorted, "Oh, you mean in response to finding out you intended to publicly reject me today? To make me look pathetic in front of the two people who saw me do the same to you ten years ago?"

He couldn't help it, his mouth fell open. How could she possibly know what he'd planned? Heat crept up his neck and his ears burned with embarrassment. She obviously knew; it would do no good to deny it. The grin on her face right now told him she'd planned the whole boyfriend scene, and that she had him in a sticky spot, hung by his own rope. Tall, dark, and definitely handsome, she'd said, and he'd desperately wanted to believe it. He had searched for some hint that she still cared for him. And so he'd played along.

But she'd known of his plan all along, and right now, instead of savouring victory, he felt like a very small man indeed. It went against his morals, the very integrity he prided himself on, and for a moment he felt like a coward.

"So what if I did? It's not like you didn't deserve it," he defended himself. He shoved his hands in his pockets, bunching his fingers together. "Twice now you've done it to me. I thought you deserved to see how it felt for once. When I got the reunion invitation, it gave me the perfect opportunity. I could make a scene and turn you away while Lisa and Jan watched."

Katie's brows pulled together in confusion. "Twice? I don't follow."

He sighed. "Ten years ago when I asked you to the prom. And at the anniversary brunch."

"At the brunch? But we were alone!" Her gaze flitted to his, distressed and uncertain. "You thought I ran because…that I took off…oh."

What was she trying to say? What other explanation was there for her behaviour? Yet she clearly looked upset that he thought she'd rejected him. He should hate her for what she'd done, but instead he thought he understood it. He was no prize. He knew it and why should he blame her for running from him?

"You left. I had to go back to the party. Everyone saw you leave, Katie, like a demon was on your heels. In a cab. Then I return and all the guests are watching me. Some with pity....poor Ric, unlucky in love....some curious about what we must have fought about. I was completely humiliated. I felt exactly like I did ten years ago when I stood by your locker and you laughed in my face."

Just once, he had to hear her admit it, even though he knew he would hate the answer. Emotion tugged at his voice, raw with anguish as he asked, "Was being with me so unbearable that you had to run away?"

"No! Of course not!"

"Then why?"

Katie stepped away from the door. The office was tiny, housing only a desk with computer terminal, a credenza with a fax/printer/copier on the top, a telephone and a small table with papers scattered on its surface. It left little room for her to move around. She put her hands on the top of the rolling desk chair, effectively making it a tangible barrier between them in the enclosed space. She hesitated in answering, while he waited expectantly, feeling as though she were putting him through the tortures of hell.

"Katie? Why would you run?" He couldn't let the matter drop. "You acted like I was going to hurt you or something."

"You were. Maybe not that particular day, but eventually. I knew it and for a while let myself forget." She paused. Ric ran his hand through his hair, frustrated. When she spoke again, her words seemed carefully measured.

"You are not repulsive, Ric. I promise you."

"I'd never hurt you, Katie."

"That's what they all say. But they always do."

He leaned back, resting his hips on the edge of the table. "They." The steel was back in his voice. "I'm assuming by that you mean my gender in general?"

"Um, yes."

He frowned. "By God, that's a generalization I don't care for. I suppose you think I'd do the same thing as what's his name. Use you for my own ends and cut you loose when it suited me?" He shook his head. "I thought you knew me better."

After a few moments, she looked up, defiant, and his heart stopped. In that one instant, she was his Katie. Katie the brave, the strong, the independent. Those were the reasons he loved her now and ironically, the reasons why she wouldn't let them be together. He loved her and hated her for them at the same time.

She turned the tables on him, angry as a mad hornet. "How can you say that, when your plan for today was to bring me down? Strip me of my dignity in the one place I've worked hard to build?" She challenged him, her tone laced with rough emotion.

"You're right. It was a horrible plan. But I didn't go through with it. I couldn't. I couldn't hurt you the way you'd hurt me. The reason I was late was because I knew I couldn't go through with it. I drove around downtown twice, wondering what I was going to do." He wanted to reach out and touch her but knew he must not. "I may not like what you've done, but I couldn't actually do something so mean and petty in retaliation. I came here planning to look after the meeting. And that's all."

He angled his head at her, curious. "But that reminds me. How did you find out about it anyway?"

"I delivered some stuff to Christine and thought I'd pop in. I didn't like how we'd left things and thought perhaps I should try to explain about the brunch."

"What's to explain? I kissed you and you ran."

"There's more to it than that." She spread her hands wide, imploring him to understand. "You assumed why, and that was your big mistake."

Had he been wrong about her? She'd already said he wasn't repulsive, but what other reason could she have had to run away? He was on the verge of thinking the impossible when she continued on.

"Anyway, you weren't in your office. I had a look at your day planner; it was sitting open on your desk. Sue me. The point is, you intended to use my weaknesses against me and I can't forgive you for that."

"You can't forgive me. Well." He straightened and stared while the fax machine rang again and paper started scrolling out. "I beg your puritanical pardon for having an inappropriate response when my feelings got hurt." The memory of holding her in his arms, of touching her, flooded back, leaving him raw and vulnerable. He sniffed, curling his top lip. "So in return you came up with your own plan to cut mine off at the knees."

"You'd look pretty stupid rejecting me when I was already involved with someone else."

"Ah." He folded his arms across his chest, hiding his relief. She wasn't seeing anyone. He'd had the feeling she was bluffing but a little part of his heart was worried she'd already moved on.

"Except you think fast on your feet. I didn't anticipate you playing along." Her fingers flexed against the black back of the chair; her smile was weak. "Then I realized I'd played right into your hands. I'd gushed about a boyfriend, you pretended to be him. It would have made your rejection of me that much more satisfying."

"Not satisfying. There's nothing to be proud of when you hurt someone else."

Her gaze met his, honest and open for the first time that afternoon. "I know." She sighed deeply.

"But you could have corrected me when I touched you. Accused me of fooling with Lisa and Jan, make it all seem like a joke. You let it go. Why?"

He held his breath waiting for her answer. *Because I wanted it to be true*, he wanted to hear her say. Despite everything, despite his vow that he was done with her, he knew that with the right answer to this one question, he'd be hers. After all she'd done, she still had that power. Perhaps because despite it all, he still sensed a vulnerability about her, and he wanted to be the one to take it away and make it right.

"I...I guess you took me by surprise, and I didn't think of it."

Oh. Well, so much for that idea. *Stupid, stupid*, he chided himself. When was he going to learn not to get his hopes up?

"So we're back to square one." He heard his own voice and it sounded oddly flat.

"Not exactly." The muted sound of the restaurant bustle behind them filtered through the door. "We have a somewhat successful business between us."

"Business." He snorted. He couldn't give a good damn about the business right now. What he had always wanted was Katie's love and she was getting further and further out of his reach. The gulf between them was growing wider by the minute, and he was tired of fighting for something that wasn't his to begin with. "Fine. I'll tell you what. I'll keep up my end of the bargain. I'll be the moneybags and you can run it however the hell you want, and we'll just stay out of each other's way as much as possible."

He was tired of the rollercoaster up and down feelings. One moment he was furious, the next tender and understanding. It wore him down. She wanted a bottom line. That was fine. Anger built in long waves inside him, and he knew he had to get out of there before he said something he would regret. He was sick and tired of dollar signs announcing his arrival and people who were only interested in the Ric Emerson who existed now, and not the person he was before. Perhaps that was part of the reason why he wanted Katie so much. She knew where he came from. She knew his childhood dreams and some of what it had cost him to achieve them.

Yet now, at this moment, it didn't seem to matter to her and he was done fighting. "I'll leave you alone to your precious business. Call me when you need a cheque."

He tried to shoulder past her but she shot out her hand, staying his departure with a grip on his arm. "What do you want from me, Ric? I told you from the beginning…"

He spun to face her. He clenched his jaw, feeling his frustration with her bubble up until he opened his mouth and it came pouring out.

"What do I want? I want you to see me. Me!" he shouted. He saw her eyes grow wide at his outburst but didn't care. "That's all I ever wanted, Katie! I'm not the high school nerd who changed his appearance and became a success. I'm not a chequebook, there to fund your precious project! I'm not that anymore than you're the party girl who never took anything seriously. I have feelings, hopes, dreams. I thought you understood that I saw that in you too. And me, being the fool that I am, expected the same from you. I thought you understood a bit of who I am. But I was way off base there!" He spread his hands wide, then dropped them. "There is more to me than *what* I am. I thought you knew that."

As his anger wore out, hurt and disappointment took its place and he knew he had to leave now. Her eyes looked up into his, and he thought for a moment he saw a hint of moisture in the blue depths.

"What about you, Ric? What do you see when you look at me?"

"You don't want to know," he whispered hoarsely.

"Yes, I think I do. I think you need to tell me, too."

He did need to tell her, and by the looks of things, he might never have another chance. It was clear to him that any hope of a personal relationship with her was gone, and before they parted ways, he wanted to tell her exactly what he thought. Clear his chest and maybe, just maybe, move on.

"I think you're hiding, and I don't think you trust anyone. I think you're insecure and hell bent on 'proving' yourself no matter what the cost to you or anyone else." He took a breath, saw her mouth drop open in shock and carried on before he lost his nerve. "I think you're egocentric and see the world as it affects you, and the hell with anyone else. I think you see things in black and white and forget that sometimes grey is as good as it gets. I think you're willing to hurt people who love you, have always loved you, to get what you want. I think you are punishing everyone else for what one person did to you. And I think your priorities are completely out of whack. You underestimate yourself and therefore everyone else does too. If you saw yourself like I do—a woman who fights for what she wants and uses hard work and determination to make it happen—you would be more sure of yourself, and proud. I wish…" he paused, dropped his head to look at the floor instead of in her wounded eyes, "I wish you had given us a chance."

"I'm sorry," she whispered, and his heart broke. For a brief, dark moment, he felt like that insecure boy ten years ago. But he wasn't Nerdboy any longer. He was stronger and better than that.

"I don't want your sympathy. Don't you get that? I never did," he choked out, yanking open the door and disappearing around the corner.

Katie locked the door behind him, sank into the desk chair, and let the tears come.

How had it come to this?

Her breath came in harsh gasps as she reached for the tissues. It had been hard to keep the truth from Ric. He'd pinned her with his eyes, and she could see he wanted her to tell him everything. Yet she couldn't. She couldn't tell him why she was scared of becoming involved with him or why succeeding at the Pick and Choose was so important. She had trusted completely once before, and look where that had gotten her. In an office not much bigger than this one, and a whole lot more humiliated. She struggled to put the memory behind her. She couldn't give anyone that power ever again...the power to take away her pride.

There was no doubt in her mind that Lisa and Jan thought Ric the force behind the Pick and Choose and Katie the hired help. Ric was dynamic and powerful. She was the back to basics, hands-on person. It wasn't what she wanted. She wanted...no, needed...her own power. Being with Ric wouldn't achieve that. She'd always be in his shadow.

He'd asked for her to look deeper, see the man he was inside, and it had taken everything she had not to turn into his arms and tell him she did. She saw who he was, but the problem was she was in love with him and by telling him that, she'd only hurt him more. She'd done enough already. If she'd told him she ran from him at the brunch because his kiss had been everything she'd ever wanted, then in the same breath told him she couldn't have a relationship with him, it would only make it harder for both of them. It was better to let him believe she was all about the business. And maybe one day, they would be able to move past it and working together wouldn't seem as difficult.

Katie wiped her eyes and sighed, sitting back in the chair with her bottom lip wobbling pitifully. He hadn't said the words either, but it didn't take a genius to figure out she'd hurt him and hurt him deeply. Or to realize that he had feelings for her that went far deeper than she'd expected.

But he didn't know everything. And Katie knew some things had to come before personal happiness. Things like the Pick and Choose and her self-respect.

Chapter Twelve

Slice carefully, slide fingers in and peel apart gently.

Katie repeated the steps in her brain to keep her mind off Ric. So far forty mini-pitas were split and in a bowl, waiting for filling. She sliced another in half, peeled the halves into pockets, and tossed them in the bowl with the others.

His words echoed through her brain far too often. *I don't want your sympathy. Don't you get that?* She sighed heavily, weighed down by regrets. Did she pity him? Had she always? The anguish in his eyes, that truth, told her he thought so. At that moment, she'd wanted to walk into his arms and tell him the whole truth. But she'd hesitated, her fear keeping her still and offering nothing more than a paltry apology. And she'd let him walk away, without telling him how she really felt.

She probably shouldn't have taken the catering job, but keeping busy these days and focusing on the Pick and Choose had become her only priority. The fact was his parting words had hit their mark. He'd never wanted her pity. Perhaps that affected her more than anything else because she understood it well. Nothing burned as badly as having your pride stripped. If he thought she felt sorry for him, then his pride would have taken the hit. And the last thing he would want from the person he cared about was pity.

"Need some help?" Jenna's voice interrupted as Katie sliced another pita.

"I've got it covered." Katie looked up and realized the lunch crowd was thinning. Karen was putting together a chili and bun combo and the new girl, Indie, was clearing tables. "Where did the time go?"

"You've been busy working yourself into the ground," Jenna stated matter-of-factly. "This is your third catering job in the past two weeks. Plus working full time at this restaurant. When do you sleep?"

I don't, Katie thought wryly, but answered, "It's good money and exposure." That much was true, at least. Word of mouth was the best publicity she could get, and if she took these small jobs, it would only benefit the Pick and Choose. She didn't say the real reason was to try to stop thinking of Ric.

Katie put the pitas aside, took a huge bowl of filling from the fridge, and began stuffing them, arranging them on a huge platter. Jenna's hand on her arm made her pause.

"Katie, we've been through a lot together. What's really going on?"

Katie looked up and saw real concern in her friend's eyes. "I'm fine." At Jenna's raised eyebrow, she insisted. "Truly I am. You don't have to stare at me that way."

Jenna shrugged. "You keep telling yourself that, babe. I know you. You're in major denial and you're working yourself to death so you don't think about him."

"About who?"

Jenna's light laugh was a breath of fresh air, and Katie couldn't help but smile in return. But she kept stuffing pitas.

"You know very well who I mean." Jenna picked up a spoon and dipped it into the bowl of cold curried chicken. "We haven't seen or heard from Ric since the day he stormed out of here."

"It's for the best."

Katie dropped her spoon in the stainless steel sink and moved to stuffing mushrooms, away from Jenna's knowing eyes. Katie didn't want to talk about Ric. It was better this way. She had always wanted to keep their relationship professional. The fact he was a very silent partner now was only a bonus.

Or it would be, if she didn't miss him so terribly. She found herself looking up with every "ding" of the bell as the door opened. His apron still lay folded neatly behind the counter, and she missed seeing him in it, a dishpan in his hands as he cleaned tables. She missed the way he crinkled his forehead when he was puzzling out the cash register, or his ready smile as he dealt with customers.

She remembered her mother saying often, "Be careful what you wish for, dear. It might come true."

It had. She'd wanted Ric to stay out of her way from the start, and now he was. Somehow the reality wasn't as great as the concept.

Jenna leaned back against the counter, the spoon in her hand forgotten. "Katie. You've been working sixteen hour days for the past two weeks. Yesterday morning I caught you scrubbing around the grout in the bathroom with a toothbrush. I don't get it. Ric's great. He's smart and handsome and obviously cares for you very much. What's the problem?"

Oh, if it were only that simple. And she didn't want to dredge up all the reasons again, when they were pointless now.

"You know my reasons, okay? Things wouldn't work between us, so it's for the best he's not around."

"My, don't you sound convincing."

Katie looked up, saw the sarcastic quirk to Jenna's lips and couldn't help grinning back. It was impossible to be angry with her. "Oh, shut up. Help me put together the spirals."

Jenna got out the tortillas while Katie mixed spread in a bowl. "You know you don't have to prove yourself to me, right, Katie?" Jenna's gaze was unconditionally supportive. "I know you've been working night and day to make this business work, but where's the line? When you start shutting out a guy like Ric, one who obviously loves you, I have to wonder."

"He's never said once he loves me." She fought against the memory of his eyes just before his lips touched hers under the birch. No, he hadn't said it, but she'd seen it, and ultimately it was why she'd run.

Jenna's snort was exasperated. "Even you're not that blind. The guy would go to the ends of the earth for you. The way he looks at you. We all see it. We'd all give our right arms for a man to look at us the way Ric looks at you."

Katie flushed. Perhaps if they hadn't started this business together. But there'd always be those who thought she'd succeeded because of Ric, that she was only riding his coattails. The timing was wrong.

Jenna sliced a tortilla, concentrating on cutting each round exactly one inch thick. "You've done what you set out to do. Now what about you?"

"Maybe I have." Katie spread filling on a tortilla and Jenna rolled it up, putting it aside. It was true, the Pick and Choose was running fabulously. Katie was particularly pleased with the new catering opportunities which had opened up. It was a side she and Ric hadn't discussed, and despite the long hours she knew it was worth it in the end. They worked silently for a few minutes until Katie added, "Maybe I'm still proving it to myself. My personal life will have to wait."

Katie garnished the pita tray with kale and parsley, avoiding Jenna's eyes. Professionally, she was finding her feet. Trusting her personal judgment was the one place she got stuck every time. She was constantly making wrong choices in her personal life. What would have happened if she'd accepted Ric's invitation to prom those years ago instead of ridiculing him? What if she'd never been involved with Craig, and had shown better judgment in the years after high school?

Would her heart still be free, instead of the way it was now, locked behind a wall of insecurity and distrust?

Jenna took off her apron and hung it on a hook by the back door. "That's a shame, then," she responded. "Because you're going to miss out on the best thing to happen to you. You can't live your life in fear, Katie."

Katie looked up, anger flaring briefly. "Fear? You don't think I had to battle fear every moment when I was starting this place? You don't think I'm scared every day that my success will vaporize? Just because things have worked out so far, doesn't mean I can sit back and rest on my laurels." The Pick and Choose was her baby, and it was flourishing. It should have been enough. But she wanted more. She wanted to be validated. She wanted the world to say, "That was a great idea, and there's the woman who made it happen." Perhaps it made her egotistical, as Ric said. But she desired that approval above all else.

Jenna's eyes softened. "I know you're scared. But you can't put a cage around your heart. At some point you're going to have to let it out. And maybe you'll get hurt. But maybe you won't. Only you can decide when you're ready to take that leap. Only you'll know when it's worth it. I hope."

Jenna went down the street for her afternoon break, leaving Katie standing behind the counter, awash in conflicting emotions and with half the catering order left to fill before five p.m.

⅋☉ ☂ℜ

Katie swatted at a mosquito as she lit the citronella torches on the perimeter of the cobbled terrace. Most of the trays were on ice, waiting for hungry guests to arrive. Pitchers of ice water sat on a side table, along with a punch bowl filled with cranberry lemonade, flower-shaped ice cubes floating on its surface. In the kitchen, plastic containers of food to replenish the trays were stacked in the fridge. Katie pressed a hand to her belly. Her other two jobs had been catering board meetings, where she simply dropped off boxes of made-to-order sandwiches and bottled drinks. This, however, was a private function. A financial group golf outing, followed by an evening repast at a home on the edge of the course. She'd pulled out her plain black trousers and tailored white blouse for the occasion. The Pick and Choose was on trial tonight, and by association, she was too. If she pulled this off, it would mean other similar functions, perhaps even a whole new side business to explore.

The host and hostess entered, approaching and shaking her hand. "Miss Buick. I see you're all set up. Fantastic. Our guests will be arriving any moment."

"Is everything to your liking? I can certainly shuffle things around."

"No, no. It looks great the way it is. This is informal, after all. Our guests will help themselves, but if you wouldn't mind manning the punch bowl for a while, and refilling the food as required."

"Of course." Katie smiled her most professional smile. If she did this right, it could lead to more catering opportunities within this social circle. "Let me know if there's anything you need."

At that moment, she heard voices and straightened the hem of her blouse as she made her way to the beverage table.

It was a small gathering of perhaps twenty, a mix of men and women dressed for golf in collared shirts, stylish sun visors and plastic spiked shoes that made thin clippy sounds on the cobbled terrace. Katie smiled and offered each guest a drink as they filtered in, feeling more and more like a poor relation as she caught snippets of conversations about venture capital and mutual funds. The finance world was not hers. It was Ric's world, and she easily pictured him in such a setting. Hers was pouring drinks and offering napkins. It was an important service, but right now it seemed below anything being discussed in the deepening twilight.

As if divined, she turned her head briefly towards the French doors, and Ric walked through them.

His gaze met hers as she held the punch ladle forgotten in her hand. He looked wonderful. He wore tan trousers that hugged his bottom and accentuated the lean length of his legs. His golf shirt was startlingly white next to the deep tan of his skin, and he wore a knit vest over top in shades of tan and deep green. The only thing missing was a putter in his hand.

She wanted to evaporate from sight. What were the chances of their business catering an event he was attending? They stood like statues, staring at each other, words from their last meeting flooding through her mind so fast she could hardly distinguish them.

I don't want your sympathy….was my kiss so repulsive….your priorities are completely out of whack…I'd never hurt you, Katie… I'll be the moneybags and you can run it however the hell you want…I wish you had given us a chance.

She dropped the ladle into the punch bowl and quickly moved to fish it out.

When she looked back, Ric had moved off to a group of three others and stood chatting with one hand in his pocket.

Katie smiled perfunctorily and handed a glass to a woman in pink and white. She snuck glances at Ric surreptitiously, watching him circulate through the room, smiling and chatting.

Eventually he made his way over to her table. "Good evening, Katie."

She looked up, keeping her expression as impersonal as she could. "Would you like some punch?"

His face clouded at her bland tone and she felt a niggle of guilt for not smiling at him. It was too difficult; there was too much between them. She didn't want the others present to know she and Ric were in business together. He was a successful big businessman and she was only the catering help tonight. If she could only stay somewhat anonymous and get through the next few hours with her pride in tact, she'd consider it a job well done.

"Punch would be nice. Getting a few catering jobs lately, huh? Why isn't Jenna here?" He took the glass she offered, looking down at her intensely and she knew he was in no hurry to move on. The fact that he still referred to their partnership sent butterflies through her belly.

"It's a bit of a side business I'm exploring. I thought it best to look after it myself." She braved a glance into his handsome face. "You're pretty much a silent partner these days."

"Whose fault is that?"

She smiled through her teeth at a passing guest, ignoring Ric's pointed question. She couldn't let herself be drawn into an argument tonight. Not when she was on the job.

"What are you doing here, Ric? It's a bit weird, don't you think? You attending a function *we're* catering?" To emphasize the sense of the absurd, she offered him a plate. "Curry pita?"

He placed one dutifully on his plate, his expression infuriatingly bland. "You didn't know? Marta asked me for a caterer. I suggested the Pick and Choose."

"You did what?" She clenched her teeth as anger raced through her and she struggled to maintain control over her emotions.

Her voice was low and threatening and his chin flattened in surprise. "Don't be angry. I knew you'd be up for the job. I told her to call you. What's the problem? It is good business."

The problem? Was he serious? He couldn't see what sort of position this put her in? Did everyone here know that Ric's latest project was providing the food? She bit down on her lip to keep from crying. It was all too much. She only got this job because of Ric. Just when she thought she was succeeding in doing things single-handedly, he ambushed her with the revelation he'd set it up. On the back of that thought was another—had he had a hand in the others as well?

She cleared her throat and struggled to keep her expression as neutral as possible. "And the others? The two jobs from last week?"

"I sit on the board for the children's charity, it's true. We had a meeting about this year's auction and ball, and I set up lunch. The other, I'm not sure." He actually looked genuinely confused at her response.

Katie gripped the punch ladle until her knuckles turned white. He didn't understand. Had never understood, or else he'd know how doing such a thing would make her feel. He had contacted the reunion committee. He'd had a direct hand in three of her four catering jobs. Even as a silent partner, he was orchestrating things from the sidelines.

"So much for control," she muttered, frenetically filling glasses with punch even though no one was waiting to drink them.

"I'm sorry?"

She lifted her chin, glaring at him. "Oh aren't you all innocence," she hissed, annoyed she couldn't light into him like she wanted. "Poor little Katie, better help her little business along. I can get my own jobs, you know!"

A few heads turned their way so she pasted on an artificial smile and plopped a skewer of grilled chicken on his plate as they moved slowly down the table.

"I'm the one with the money behind this venture. I can't believe you'd have a problem with getting business and boosting profits."

"Oh, I don't." Her lips curved up sweetly. "It's your methods I have issues with. The last I heard, you were going to let me run the business and you were going to write the cheques."

His expression soured and regret tempered her feeling of victory. She hadn't meant to bring up all the hurtful things that were said at their last meeting. Why couldn't he go away and stay there? Eventually all her feelings would go away, too, and they'd both be happy. All she wanted was to stand on her own two feet, make her business a success and collect the accolades from those who said she could never do it. It would have been much better if he'd agreed to a simple loan and regular payments rather than demanding to be involved at every step from inception to the day to day operations. She scanned the room. Everyone here probably thought she, not the Pick and Choose, was

Ric's little project. How was she ever going to be taken seriously if he kept derailing all her attempts at complete independence?

"I beg your pardon for helping." He treated her to a scathing glare. "In case you've forgotten, my bottom line is the same as yours. Keep the Pick and Choose in the black. Don't yell at me if you have other agendas."

Her hands landed on her hips. "Don't you dare question my motives! Not you, Mr. Master Schemer!"

The room quieted.

Oh, great. Katie stepped back, biting her tongue in her haste to shut her mouth. Ric's cheeks stained red through his tan. Not only had Ric influenced her business, but he'd drawn her into a public scene. Out of the corner of her eye, she saw a few knowing smiles, no doubt assuming it was a lover's quarrel. Oh, why couldn't he leave her alone to run her business in peace?

"If you'll excuse me, I have food to replenish," she offered haughtily, pleased it came out in a snobby, dismissive tone.

"That's fine. I'm done here." His tone was so final she blinked. The wave of his hand told her to proceed, and collecting her empty trays, she escaped to the kitchen.

She swung through the galley doors, tears pricking behind her eyes as her stomach trembled with barely contained emotion. What was it about his censure that tore her apart every time? Why on earth did his opinion of her matter so much?

She swallowed the lump in her throat, dumping the trays in a heap on the counter. Because she loved him, that was why. And he kept walking away. *But I keep pushing him*, a voice inside her argued.

She knew why, even though the reason seemed to be getting weaker with every miserable day without him in her life.

But according to him, it didn't matter anymore anyway. He was done, and now she should focus on moving on. The problem was despite the fact he was through with her, her heart didn't seem to be listening.

She busied herself refilling the food. Keeping busy would keep the evening moving much faster. Everywhere she looked she saw Ric. She heard his voice through the threads of conversations that filtered in faintly from outside. The sun sank lower in the sky and the terrace was lit by the flickering flame of the torches keeping mosquitoes at bay.

The hostess snuck in for a moment. "Katie," she said with a smile, "the comments on the food are very complimentary. Thanks for doing such a great job."

"I'm happy they like it. Good for me, and good for you."

"I thought you'd like to know everyone seems to be enjoying it."

"Then perhaps you'll keep me in mind for other functions." Katie put down her plastic storage container and reached into her pocket for a business card. "I'm very flexible with choices and settings; whatever you need, please feel free to call." She handed the card to Marta, grinding her teeth to keep her smile in place. Perhaps they'd all taken in the scene with Ric, but above all Katie was there to promote her business and she'd swallow any amount of pride to do it.

"Ric said you were tenacious." Marta laughed, making Katie unsure whether to be relieved or chagrined. Double damn him for making her look unprofessional. "Next time perhaps we won't include entertainment in the contract, hmm?"

"No, ma'am," Katie replied, relieved when Marta's eyes twinkled at her mischievously.

Marta waved the card in the air before putting it in her pocket. "I think he's finally met his match," she threw out as she returned to her guests.

In a pig's eye. Katie's polite smile fled the moment her employer was out the door. He'd engineered things for the last time. She'd make sure of it. She shouldn't have thrown such a scene about his help, and for that he deserved an apology. His intentions had probably been good all along, and she was the one with the problem. She needed to explain to him why she felt such a need to be independent. Pressing a hand to her belly, she fought against the fear that centred there. Hopefully, he would understand. They couldn't remain business partners with the way things were now. They needed to work this out so they could at least maintain a civil working relationship.

Feeling better, she was carrying the pitas and mushrooms in her hands, the dip balanced between the trays, when she entered through the open French doors and saw Ric talking to a woman she hadn't seen previously.

Katie halted, her feet suddenly heavy as lead as the woman laughed and placed her hand on Ric's arm. The sharp dagger of jealousy passed through her. She had no right to feel envious. She'd turned Ric away at every opportunity, and even with Lisa, she'd been angry and annoyed but not particularly jealous. But now, seeing this woman leaning against Ric's arm, she hated her just for existing.

The woman said something that made Ric smile, turned to the side, and Katie almost dropped her trays in shock.

Patricia. Patricia Logan was draped over Ric's arm. And he was hanging on her every word.

Patricia suddenly seemed to notice her standing there and when their eyes met, Katie shrank to two inches tall. Sensing her dominance, Patricia bared her teeth in what could only be interpreted as a victorious smile. She looked down her nose before turning her back on Katie completely, effectively shutting her out physically and personally from the group.

The line had been drawn. Guests versus the hired help, and Katie knew exactly where she belonged in that moment.

Woodenly she retreated, putting the trays of food in their proper place. She fiddled with tiny things to keep her hands busy. Of all the events to cater. Patricia *and* Ric, all in one night. And they knew each other. Before the end of the night, he'd know the whole sordid story...or at least Patricia's version of it. It was the only version that mattered.

Her cheeks flamed. It was only right, she supposed. It was the price she had to pay for being stupid and gullible.

I don't know why you're being so nice, she's not worth it.

Those words, delivered in Patricia's haughty voice, had haunted her for two years. Not worth it, not worth it. It had almost become a mantra.

This was a nightmare. Was there no way to escape the past? The one woman Katie hoped she never had to meet again was here, and chatting most pleasantly to Ric. She couldn't believe they were acquainted. Ric couldn't possibly be friends with such a self-absorbed viper. She watched them talking, her heart pounding so loudly she was sure everyone could hear it.

His laugh reached her through the deepening evening. Ric would finally know the rest of the story. He'd know that not only had Craig humiliated her personally, as she'd revealed, but that Craig had conspired with Patricia to have her arrested.

Her stomach twisted at the ignominy of it all—the police coming into O'Neill's and actually handcuffing her, taking her out in front of patrons, sitting in the ugly grey room at the police station while she waited for her parents to come pick her up. A few hours later, Craig coming in with Patricia and making himself look good by asking for mercy on her part.

"I don't know why you're being so nice, she's not worth it," Patricia had condescended.

"She made a mistake," he'd replied, his eyes smug with victory. "She won't make it again. Better to be rid of her than face a time-consuming court case," he'd added, and Patricia had all but latched on his arm. In one move, he'd covered his own embezzling butt and got the girl.

Katie hadn't forgiven him the betrayal or the damage to her personal reputation. She'd never had a chance to rebut the charges, since they'd been dropped. Her only revenge had been trying to prove them wrong.

Patricia remained close to Ric's side and Katie's heart slipped further and further into despondency as the minutes ticked by. He surely knew by now. She had no proof she hadn't done it. And he'd be regretting ever getting involved with her or her fledgling business. Any plan she had to talk to him about tonight would be moot now. She placed a hand on her forehead wearily. First Ric, and now Patricia. This was turning into the night from hell. What would his reaction be? Would he back out of their partnership?

She began picking up the remains of the evening, packing leftovers into foil pans for the hostess. Regrets piled on her conscience with each silver tray she stacked. She should have treated him better all those years ago. She shouldn't have been so naïve. She should have turned down his offer for partnership. She should have stayed away from that silly family brunch. She should have...

That's enough shoulds for anyone, she realized, squaring her chin. Too many mistakes had been made. It was time she went about fixing them, once and for all.

Chapter Thirteen

Ric stared at the papers with disbelief.

Never in a million years had he thought she'd go this far, but she had. He sat heavily in his chair, resting his elbows on his desk. Katie had taken steps to dissolve their partnership. The brown envelope had been messengered this morning. All he had to do was sign. A lawyer—her lawyer, not Mark—had drawn up papers. His investment was protected. She was repaying the capital he'd invested, at a fair rate of interest. His eyebrows furrowed as the papers shook in his hands. Those payments, taken from the profits of the Pick and Choose, added on to expenses and the salary of her employees, would leave next to nothing for Katie to live on.

How would she manage?

Not my problem, he thought quickly, but sighed heavily. Sure it was. He loved her as much now as he ever had. The way she'd stood up to him at Marta's the other night…she was fiery and passionate about her pride. He'd wanted her to translate that fire into passion for him too, but his plan had failed. Instead he'd ruined the whole thing by trying to take things further than he should have at the brunch. That day had been the beginning of the downhill slide for them.

His index finger rubbed his bottom lip as he scanned the legalese. He'd only been trying to help by lining up a few catering jobs. He hadn't thought it a bad thing to set up a few gigs for her. Correction. For them. Only now there was no *them*. There was only Katie, running her business on her own, and Ric, sitting in his office, their relationship condensed down to payment terms and interest rates.

He turned his back on the desk and paced, growing angrier by the second. Did she honestly think he was only concerned about recouping his investment? Didn't she understand he had more at stake—like his feelings for her, and the sense of fulfillment he got from his involvement in the restaurant? He tapped the sheaf of papers together and slid them back into the envelope. He was not the boy he'd been ten years ago. That boy had let her walk away, no questions asked, no fight. With a blind acceptance that he wasn't the type she could ever care about.

Well, he wasn't that boy any longer. Ric's fingers dug into the envelope as he pocketed his car keys. This wasn't over. He wasn't going to walk away from her so easily this time. If she expected him to simply sign and leave her and the business they'd built together, she was sadly mistaken. He thought he'd said everything that afternoon at the Pick and Choose. But he hadn't. There was more she needed to know.

ଞ ଔ

A magazine, or the television?

Katie debated between the two, needing something mindless to do to wind down. The day had been busy, busier than most. Things had slowed at the Pick and Choose now summer was over, but today it seemed as if everyone in a ten block radius decided to have lunch at her restaurant. Added to that, her body was tensed with permanent anxiety about Ric and how he'd react to the documents she'd couriered this morning. All afternoon, she'd expected him to storm into the Pick and Choose, demanding to know what she meant. Every time the door opened or the phone rang, her heart took a little leap of fear and anticipation.

Yes, she acknowledged. Anticipation. Despite how complicated everything had become, he still had that power over her. It puzzled her. After all, he'd hurt her and she fought with him every step of the way, trying to be independent.

She sank on to the sofa, pushing the red button on the remote. The opening scenes of a popular forensics show flashed on the screen but she didn't pay attention. Ric hadn't come. Which meant he probably was signing the document and messengering it back to her lawyer even now.

It was the right thing to do. It was. Just because it made her feel miserable didn't mean it wasn't right.

He'd tried to control and manipulate the business from the very beginning. He'd even tried to manipulate her. She watched the screen blindly as the coroner and his assistant pulled the sheet back on a stiff, grey body. If Ric signed the papers, that complication would be gone and she could concentrate on building her business. If things went well, maybe she could even open a second location within a year or two.

If only she could forget his kiss, the way his arms felt around her, the scent of his cologne and hair gel mingled together as they swayed gently to the music.

She stood abruptly. Thoughts like that were crazy, especially now. It was over between them, over with a capital "O". It was how it had to be and that was that.

She fled into the kitchen, grabbing a spoon and heading for the freezer. Tonight was no night for the lite soy frozen dessert crap. She reached towards the back and took out the high test, premium ice cream. Dipping her spoon, she came up with a mixture of vanilla, chocolate fudge chunks and peanuts.

"Mmm." It wasn't quite the same, but a close substitute to his rich, silky voice and warm chocolaty eyes.

Oh, who was she kidding, she thought, sucking another mouthful off the spoon. It was time to face the truth and herself. She knew in her heart Ric hadn't been trying to control the business by setting up those catering jobs. He'd been trying to help. And really, why shouldn't he? It was his business too, and he had every right to promote it when he saw an opportunity.

Neither had he been wrong about the location, and so what if he owned the building? He'd never tried to strong-arm her, except for that first night when he'd proposed the partnership instead of a loan. The fact was, she knew ninety-nine percent of the problem was herself and her own hang-ups and it was time she admitted it to herself. She was so determined to prove herself that she refused to accept help and questioned every motive. She'd been unfair; she'd hurt him and hurt herself in the process.

Suddenly sick of the ice cream, she put the lid back on the carton and put it back in the freezer. It didn't matter now. He had to know now that she'd been arrested and he was likely disappointed in her and angry she hadn't told him the truth. What a mess she'd made of everything. Yes, moving on, dissolving their partnership, was the best thing to do.

The security buzzer blared through the silence. She jumped, pressing a hand to her heart. She hit the call button with a shaky finger. "Hello?"

"It's Ric."

Her finger flew off the button as if burned. Oh lord. She wasn't ready for this now. She had a drip of ice cream on her T-shirt and she was wearing sweatpants a size too large. She put her hand up to her hair—just as she suspected. A rat's nest piled on her head, bits and pieces falling out of the plain white clip she'd put in.

The buzzer rang again…oh goodness, she'd left him standing there while she panicked.

Not trusting herself to answer, she pressed the button to open the security door, released it, and took a deep breath for fortitude.

His knock came less than ten seconds later and she opened the door with a trembling hand. "Ric," she greeted, her voice flat.

He didn't even offer a greeting, but pushed past her into the apartment, through to the living room and slapped the envelope on the dining table.

She followed at a cautious distance. "So you got them."

His face was tight with anger, his lips thin as he answered. "You're crazy if you think I'm signing these!"

His belligerent tone was all she needed to get fired up. "Yes, of course. I forgot we must always do it your way!"

"If you think you can brush me off like you did ten years ago, you're sadly mistaken! I won't be discarded because I'm inconvenient!"

"I never said you were inconvenient," she retorted. "The last I remember you said you would write the cheques and I'd run the business. This is simply making those terms official." She folded her hands in front of her waist.

"The Pick and Choose is mine too! You're not the only one who invested time and energy into it. And you're not the only one who deserves credit for getting it off the ground."

"And that's why I got a lawyer to draft the papers," she contradicted rationally. "In the beginning, I thought it was understood that the restaurant would remain mine. I'm only clarifying our positions."

"By God, that sounds almost logical." He crossed his arms in front of his chest, glaring. "Except you forgot I might actually have feelings about it."

She sighed heavily, pressing her hands to her cheeks. Why couldn't he just sign them and they could both move on? She hadn't the energy for a big blow out fight. He was right, she was wrong. He should be glad to be rid of her.

"It's better this way. All we do is argue." She braved a look up. "You deserve a better partner, someone who doesn't always question your motives."

Ric began pacing the tiny space, agitated, lengthy steps while Katie watched with surprise as the usually eloquent Ric Emerson tried to find words. When he finally stopped, what he said was so shocking it rocked her to her toes.

"I love you."

Her breath caught in her chest. "What did you say?"

A twisted smile crawled up his cheek. "Go ahead and torture me by making me repeat it." He shoved his hands in his pockets. "I said I love you. Neuroses and all."

She looked down to hide her burgeoning tears, but her eyes fell on his feet.

Sandals. It was September and he was wearing cargo shorts and sandals. Looking at his bare toes, she started to laugh, remembering that day at his house and how the sight of his naked feet had turned her on.

"What's so funny?" His voice had an edge to it; and she realized he'd told her he loved her and she'd inappropriately responded by laughing.

She lifted her head, wiping away the tears and giggling a little at the same time. "Your feet. You've got the sexiest feet on the planet."

He looked down at the objects of her worship. "My feet? You are warped."

When he looked up again, she stared at him tenderly, loving the crooked smile that tilted his lips slightly to the right.

"I'm sorry," she whispered. "I'm sorry I've made things so very difficult for you. I don't want to fight with you. You deserve a partner with fewer issues. You have to understand, it was never about you."

He closed the distance between them. "God, I know that. I didn't understand for a while, but I do now. All I needed to do was put myself in your shoes to understand why you felt you needed to protect yourself."

"I duped you into financing me. There are things you didn't know, and I didn't disclose." It was a frightening and liberating thing to admit it.

"I know. They had you arrested for theft."

"How long have you known?" Her heart drummed frantically as she asked it. Surely he hadn't known before talking to Patricia.

"About the arrest? I've always known." His eyes were kind, too kind. "I did a background check before I ever drew up the contract."

"And you never said anything. You gave me the money anyway." Incredulous, her mouth fell open. She couldn't help but ask, "Why?"

"I knew you didn't do it," he stated unequivocally. "I was waiting for you to trust me enough to tell me yourself."

Something blossomed in Katie then. Something small, a seed of validation, growing from her core and spreading outward with its warmth.

It was faith. She'd hurt his feelings terribly when they were teenagers, and hadn't seen him for ten years. But faced with the facts about her, he had believed her innocent. No questions asked. Willing to put his name on the line despite the smear on her own reputation. What sort of a man did that?

The kind who trusted her and believed in her, only she'd abused that trust and faith so many times it was something else on the list of things she didn't deserve.

"I didn't trust you, and for that I'm sorry. More sorry than you'll know. I know you were only helping when you lined up those catering jobs." Her eyes implored him to understand.

"I never wanted to control you." He reached out to her and took her hand, creating a living link between them. "I know it must have looked that way. Especially after the way I acted after the brunch. There's no excuse for my behaviour. It was childish and petty and I'm not proud of it."

"You're the most honest, ethical person I know," she whispered, squeezing his fingers. "To drive you to do that, I must have really hurt you. I never wanted anyone to get hurt," she said thickly.

"Then don't do this," he implored her. "Don't ask me to leave the Pick and Choose. Don't ask me to leave you."

Oh, why did it have to be so difficult? They were making so much progress here, but if they wanted a personal relationship, it would be better to keep the professional separate. Why couldn't they each be successful in their own right, and meet on equal ground?

"I think it would be better for us if we kept business and personal separate. Don't you know how confusing this has been for me? I wanted to tell you the truth so badly that afternoon in my office."

"About the arrest."

"No." She took her hand away from his. "About why I left your parent's anniversary party. I ran from you at the brunch because when you kissed me, I...I knew I was in too much danger of letting my heart rule my head. I wanted you so much...and I vowed not to let blind trust take over my life again." Her neck drooped. "I don't trust myself, you see.

"You wanted me."

"You sound surprised. You shouldn't be. I've wanted you for a long time, Ric. Almost since the beginning."

The words echoed through the apartment, over the drone of the TV, sinking in to both of them. Katie's lower lip quivered. "Oh, I'm so tired of fighting."

"Then don't." Ric's reply was a husky whisper that sent chills down her spine. "Don't make me leave. We can run it together."

"I'd ruin it. If you want it so bad, you can buy out my half and I'll start another business."

Ric stepped backward at the suggestion, surprised. The Pick and Choose to himself, while she moved on? The thought hadn't crossed his mind, and he'd never feel right knowing he was profiting from her work. Besides, the restaurant wouldn't seem the same without her energy and commitment. She was what made it special.

"Katie, no. I'm not letting you get away this time. I did that ten years ago. I just accepted the situation and moved on. I'm not doing that now. I'm not walking away from you."

"I walked away from you, remember?" She met his eyes squarely, despite the fact her cheeks flushed with embarrassment.

"I let one conversation ruin our friendship. I let it hurt me instead of seeing it for what it was."

"And I was unspeakably callous with your feelings, rather than standing up for what I knew was the right thing."

"Are we going to trade blame all night?" He attempted a laugh but it fell flat. "Please. There has to be a way for us to work this out."

"I don't see how," she answered. "I want to be with you, Ric, but I'm still afraid to mix business with…with…"

"Pleasure?" He slid closer, whispering the word in her ear, feeling her shiver against him. Taking a risk, he placed his hand on the hollow of her back, pulling her the few inches closer he needed and laying his lips on hers. "Like this?" he murmured, softly molding her lips beneath his until he felt her resistance melt. He dragged his mouth from hers and bent at the knees so he could trace tiny kisses along her jaw and down the side of her neck. Her body was warm and yielding, so right in his arms at last, a willing participant. His hand drifted lower, over the soft fabric of her sweatpants, gripping the buttock beneath.

She moaned against him and he knew that whatever his attachment to the Pick and Choose, if he were forced decide between the restaurant and Katie, there was no contest. Business was business. Love was for a lifetime.

"I'll sign," he said against her ear. Her chest rose and fell heavily against his and he knew it was the right thing. "If it's the only way I can have you, I'll sign."

She pulled away sharply, putting a few feet of distance between them. "You're not thinking with your brain right now."

"It'll be all yours," he confirmed, his heart sinking. "You'll no longer be The Girl Most Likely to Have Fun. You'll be Katie Buick, Businesswoman and Girl Most Likely to Succeed."

"Thank you, thank you for doing this!" Katie rushed forward to hug him, beaming.

Whatever the sense of loss he felt at dissolving their association, it was more than made up for by her happiness.

Saying nothing, he took the pen she handed him, took the papers out of the envelope, and signed his name by the "x".

Partners no more.

He put down the pen and she came forward, snuggling against his chest and pressing a kiss to the hollow of his neck. He dipped down, willingly accepted her kiss, yet somehow feeling he'd lost.

Katie's heart thumped heavily against her chest as Ric's lips touched hers again. After the way the day had started out...to end it like this...with her own business, her own! and Ric too... It really was true. Sometimes you could have everything.

The shrill of the telephone opened his eyes, and with a coy smile at him, Katie reached for the cordless unit.

"Oh my God." Her breath hitched and her eyes widened as the speaker on the other end battered her with short, clipped details.

"I'll be right there," she replied, hitting the talk button on the phone. "We've gotta go," she said, her voice shrill with panic. "The Pick and Choose is on fire."

$\wp \; \text{Cg}$

When they arrived, the red circling lights of the fire tankers were swirling through the darkness on Stephen Avenue. Ric put the car in park as Katie numbly crawled out the door, leaning against the frame for support. Her eyes closed in despair. It was gone. The Pick and Choose was burning and she was powerless to stop it.

Tears ran cold down her cheeks, stinging from the acrid smoke puffing from the wreckage. Why had she thought she could do this? Why had she bothered? Her dream, her heart, was in that building. Her pride and her self-worth were on fire and would soon be nothing but soggy ashes, a pale reminder of what she'd tried to accomplish.

And failed.

She shut the car door, standing well back from the heat of the fire. Ric got out, came up behind her and said nothing, just stood at her back, his hands on her shoulders as they stared into the flames. Vehicles were prohibited on the pedestrian avenue, but this late at night, and at this moment, she didn't care. A policeman approached, asking her to move, but when she explained she was the owner, he offered his apologies and moved on, keeping an eye on the small crowd who had gathered.

Gathering her arms about herself, she gazed ahead at the building that had housed all her hopes. God, the hours of work, the plans. All gone now. How had it happened? This was her responsibility. Mentally she raced through the details of closing. Had she shut down the grill properly? Locked the back delivery door? Indie had gone out back for a cigarette—had Katie missed the butt in a garbage can? Details were a tangled mess writhing in her distraught mind. How didn't matter now, only that it was gone. Moments ago, she'd had everything. And in an instant, everything changed.

She'd been stupid to think she could handle something of this magnitude. Everyone had been right. She had failed utterly. Her body felt strangely empty as she admitted it to herself. An ash floated down on the air, landing on the ground beneath her feet. She'd reached too high, and now the fall was breaking her heart. Just when the Pick and Choose became hers, it was ripped from her.

"Katie."

His voice, saying her name, made her weep. Full sobbing, not the shocked tears of disappointment but the hard bitter ones of defeat. She was beaten and she knew it, and all she could do was let herself sink into his arms, allowing him to hold her while she cried.

His hand was warm on her hair as he cradled her head. "I'm sorry, I'm so sorry," he repeated over and over as the fire crews focused on keeping the fire contained to the Pick and Choose building alone.

He felt good. Strong, stable. Her universe, her legacy, was crumbling before her eyes, and he alone was a solitary pillar of support, the one thing keeping her from sinking completely.

As seconds ticked into minutes, the tears tapered a bit but her throat was raw and cracked from smoke and distress. Pulling away from his arms, she turned towards the building and stared at it, unseeing.

"I'll never be able to pay you back now," she said numbly. Millions of thoughts ran screaming through her head…it was gone…she owed him thousands of dollars…how did it start…they couldn't possibly be together now…

Ric's hand gripped her arm and turned her roughly to face him, his jaw set stubbornly. "Do you think I give a good goddamn about the money right now?"

"You should! I do!"

His hand dug into her elbow. "I couldn't care less about the money. I'm worried about you! You're white as a ghost!" He dipped at the knees, his gaze probing hers. "You look shell shocked. You should sit down."

She shook off his arm and moved a few steps off. "I should have known better. When the banks turned me down, I should have accepted it and moved on. Instead I went to you. Now look where it got me."

Her voice, hoarse and defeated, rose above the hiss and rush of the water from the hoses. "All the work, the months of planning, the dream, literally gone up in smoke. I reached way beyond my limits and now I'm paying for it."

"That's the biggest load of bull I've ever heard."

She spun on her heel. "I know when I'm done. Look at that." She swept her arm towards the building, glowing dully in the night. "Look at it," she wailed, choking on the words. "I am done. I failed! End of story! Everyone was right after all!"

"Stop it!" He stepped forward, gripping her upper arms in his hands and giving her a shake. Her eyes widened as her mouth dropped open in surprise. "I don't want to hear you say that again, do you hear me? You are not a failure!"

She looked down from the unconditional support in his eyes, so overwhelmed the tears threatened again. "If it looks like a duck and quacks like a duck…"

"You believed in this place when no one else would. You believed in yourself enough to know you could get it off the ground. And you were right!"

They stood side by side now, looking into the flames that were quickly destroying the business that tied them together.

"It doesn't matter now," she replied flatly. "The Pick and Choose is gone, and so is any reason for us to be in contact. You've already signed the papers. I'm sorry I dragged you into my little drama. I didn't mean for people to get hurt."

He walked away, pressing his hands to the side of his head. When he finally turned back, his lips were set in a firm line.

"The papers haven't been filed yet. We find a new location and we rebuild."

A hysterical laugh bubbled out of her chest before she could stop it. "Now who's inhaled too much smoke?"

He took two hurried steps to her and clasped her hands in his. She had to turn away from the hope on his face; it broke her heart to see it there.

"We'll take the insurance money and set up shop somewhere else. And it'll be even better."

"I can't." And she pulled away.

"Why?"

"Because it would still be you, bailing me out."

"You look at the Pick and Choose and only see the death of your dream. Only see failure. You place your value at what others have seen in the past instead of what you've earned. And I'm getting tired of it!"

"Ric, I…" But he cut her off before she could protest.

"You're wrong. It wouldn't be me bailing you out, as you put it. The Pick and Choose was always you." She tried to pull away but he refused to let her go. "I know I seemed heavy-handed at times. I controlled the money and I influenced decisions. But when you weigh those against all that you did, I had a very small part in this business.

"You bought the equipment, set up suppliers, decorated, did the hiring, the cooking, and most of the books. Do you know how fun it was for me to watch you make it come together? You knew what you wanted and you went about getting it. I loved stopping in here and helping because it made me feel a part of this incredible venture you'd put together. It made me feel alive and energized. I haven't felt so excited about business in a long time."

He tipped up her chin so that she was looking him dead in the eyes, and what she saw there was truth. "I never tried to take it over. I was only trying to help because I wanted so desperately to be a part of what you created. I wanted to be near you. I wanted you to see I was invested personally because I love you."

Her mouth opened and closed like a fish taking in water. He loved her. Her head reeled with it even as her heart rejoiced.

"Speechless for once?"

"Shut up," she murmured, pulling him close and pressing her lips to his.

He took all she offered, demanded more.

Her tongue twined with his and the sharp taste of smoke mellowed with chocolate and woman. Her hands reached around him, running over his shoulder blades and he pulled her close, close, so that a hair wouldn't fit between them. Acceptance, rich, full and freely given was heady and his head reeled with the thought that Katie finally saw him for who he was. He broke of the kiss reluctantly, cupping her jaws in his hands. "Tell me."

"I love you too, Ric." After the words were out she smiled, a joyous celebration lighting up her face like a firecracker. "I do. I'm sorry I didn't trust you...when you've been the one person I could count on."

"I understand why. You couldn't trust anyone. Then when I came up with that stupid plan for Lisa and Jan...all your doubts were confirmed. I'm very sorry about that."

He kissed her again, a short stamp of apology.

Her hand lifted softly to his cheek and he closed his eyes, reveling in the simple touch. The sweet sound of her voice washed over him as the fire crews began preparing to depart.

"I was angry with you at the golf outing. After you left the only thing I had was the business. I was proud for lining up those catering gigs. I mean I really felt a sense of accomplishment knowing I'd developed this side thing on my own. To find out it was all because of you...even after I sent you away you were affecting my life. I knew the only way to get over you was to cut all ties. Even then, it didn't work. It's time I faced up to the fact I've been unfair to you. I'd be honoured to be your business partner again."

He stared into her eyes. "You're sure?"

"Don't you know what you've become?" She clasped his wrists in her fingers, meeting his gaze squarely. "I've always been the girl who didn't take care with your feelings, and went on to be nothing special. But you are special, Ric. More than you know. More than I deserve. You always have been."

"Never say that again. You deserve everything. You picked yourself up and made something of yourself no matter what people said. That takes courage and vision and brains. Don't let anyone tell you different."

The fire chief approached, his face dusky from smoke. "You're the owners?"

Ric and Katie faced him; whatever news he had they would stand together to hear it.

"Eye witnesses report seeing a group of kids hanging around the back, and we think the fire started in the dumpster. We'll finish our investigation, of course, but I thought you'd like to know it doesn't appear to have started in your kitchen."

Katie held out her hand. "That's good to know. I appreciate the heads up."

He pulled off his glove and shook her hand. "You're welcome. You'll receive our final findings, of course."

The fire trucks pulled out, leaving a small crew to deal with hot spots. It was final. The Pick and Choose was a chunk of charred rubble, tiny flumes of smoke puffing up from random spots in the gutted building.

She took a few steps closer and snuggled up to Ric's ribs, prompting him to put his arm around her, tight to his side. She sighed. Suddenly it didn't matter what the world thought. The fire wasn't her fault. The facts were that she'd come up with this concept and did whatever it took to put it in motion. Her hard work wasn't something to be forgotten and dismissed because something had happened beyond her control. Big deal if she'd had a little help along the way. Ric had helped because he believed in her. And somewhere along the way he'd stolen her heart as well. Knowing he loved her too made her feel, for the first time, cherished and protected.

"You know what?" The words were muffled against his chest.

"Hmm?" His answer rumbled, and she felt the vibration purr into her.

Pulling away, she smiled up at him. "I don't care anymore about The Girl Most Likely to Succeed. There's something I want to be more."

"What's that?"

"The Girl Most Likely to Love You. If that's agreeable, of course."

"Should I draw up a contract? His lips curved up even as his gaze tenderly warmed her. "Make it official?"

She laughed. "That sounds good." She stared into the hissing mess of the fire. "So where do we go now?"

Ric tilted his head, pressing a kiss to her hair. "How about home?"

Katie angled her head, rubbing her cheek against his chin. "Home?"

His lips pressed against her cheek and she smiled in return at his words. "It's been waiting for you, you know. If you can deal with Gilligan's jealousy."

Tears sprung into her eyes as she was faced with the fulfillment of dreams she'd never even known existed. His house, waiting for her to come and make it a home. Perhaps even a few children. But wait...

"What about the restaurant?"

Ric pulled away, scanning the dark windows of Stephen Avenue. "Well, how about there?" He nodded at a shop down the block, on the opposite side of the street, with a leasing company's "For Lease" sign sitting in the window.

"It's close. Our clientele won't even have a problem finding us."

"And, a bonus. I don't own it."

She laughed, so full of contentment and peace that it flowed out of her. "With both our names on the lease."

His expression sobered. "Later," he whispered. "You still haven't said whether or not you'll come home with me."

"How's this for an answer?" she replied, and stood on tiptoe to tease him with her mouth.

"Mmm," she murmured, standing back and smiling at him saucily. "That's much better than ice cream."

"It had better be," he grumbled, catching her in his arms.

"I promise," she said, vowing never to let him get away again.

About the Author

To learn more about Donna, please visit www.donnaalward.com.
Send an email to Donna at mailto:donna@donnaalward.com or visit
her blog at http://www.donnaalward.blogspot.com.

Look for these titles

Coming Soon:

Almost a Family

Printed in the United States
67306LVS00002B/304-318